DEAD ZERO

SEAN PLATT
JOHNNY B. TRUANT

We greatly appreciate you taking the time to read our work. Please consider leaving a review wherever you bought the book, or telling your friends about it, to help us spread the word.

Thank you for supporting our work.

To YOU, the reader.

Thank you for taking a chance on us.

Thank you for your support.

Thank you for the emails.

Thank you for the reviews.

Thank you for reading and joining us on this road.

ONE

Like Characters From a Fairy Tale

WHEN HE FIRST SAW THE thing in his driveway, Jaron Giordina assumed his children were being assholes.

It was really no surprise. Things had always been this way. Len, the eldest, had been born on Leap Day as if to provoke his father's OCD. Jaron had a blotter on his desk with a Cross pen set. The pen set had to be squared perfectly to the blotter. The blotter, in turn, needed to square with his collection of framed photos, his In/Out basket, and the Quote-a-Day calendar his nephew had gotten him for Christmas. When Len was born on February 29th, Jaron immediately started wondering how his birthdate might complicate his need for order and tidy loose ends.

A lot, it turned out — at least by Jaron's standards. A surprising number of electronic forms turned out not to have February 29th as an option, but that wasn't even the worst of it. Right from the start, Jaron dreaded how he'd handle the issue of Len's age. On his third March 1st, everyone agreed Len turned two — but it bothered Jaron that on the boy's "birthday," he was *technically, sorta* "two years and one day" instead. There was nothing orderly about it.

Amber had arrived shortly after Len turned three. The girl was a cat burglar and a cock-blocker. Not only could she get out of her crib and defeat all the baby-proofing Jaron and May threw at her, but she also timed her nighttime excursions for the occasions when Jaron and May were down to get frisky. If they had a nickel for every time their daughter arrived at the bedside during foreplay to ask Mommy and Daddy where her favorite toys had gone, the family would have at least enough nickels to buy a cage for the little brat.

So when Jaron discovered the tall and tattered thing in his driveway one evening after sunset, he assumed it was a Halloween decoration. May and the kids had dragged fake cobwebs over the bushes the weekend before and had even added an enormous spider whose legs wrapped the pillars. Len wanted to buy one of those welcome mat phantoms he'd seen in the Halloween Store to go with it. A seven-foot animatronic Grim Reaper that screamed and leaped whenever some poor schmuck stepped on a pressure-sensitive mat. Jaron said he vetoed the thing because it would make the neighborhood kids wet their pants (a plus in Len's book), but the real reason was that it made *him* want to wet *his* pants, too. Jaron the Orderly was no fan of scares.

But now this had happened. Len and Amber must have manipulated May while he'd been at work. Now Jaron would have to deal with the horror in front of his home for two weeks or more. He'd have to use the garage to avoid it when he went out for walks, and he'd have to do it sneakily if he didn't want his family to ridicule him. Either way, he sure as hell wasn't going to go anywhere near it.

But of course, it was dark when Jaron got home from work and made his discovery, and the thing in the driveway was far more disturbing in the shadows than in daylight. Of course, the garage never had enough room for a car, so Jaron had to park in the driveway. And of course, May, who'd gone over his head to buy this pants-piss-inducer, had occupied the left side, leaving the right side open … adjacent to the Grim Reaper.

At least it was on his passenger side. At least he could slide out, then scamper for the door without having to walk within—

(Oh, just say it.)

—within *reaching distance* of the stupid, horrible thing.

But by the time Jaron made it to the garage, something not-quite-right was rattling inside his skull. Hadn't the Grim Reaper been taller in the Halloween Store? And hadn't its cloaks been sleek black, not shabby gray? It'd had a hood, not hair. And hadn't Jaron seen the thing moving?

No. No, you definitely did not see it moving.

He didn't want to look back, despite the inconsistencies. And he wouldn't have, except that the idea of *not* doing so was suddenly much more horrifying. Jaron had dropped the keys into his pocket, but the door, after dark, would be locked. He'd have to dig them back out or ring the bell. Either way would allow plenty of time for Death to come up from behind and tap him on the shoulder.

Jaron knew how this worked. He'd been made to see horror movies before.

He waited for the motion sensor on the porch

light to brighten his way, but that piece of shit had never worked right. He forced himself to turn.

Of course, the Grim Reaper was near the begonias instead of where he'd last seen it.

Jaron shrieked, dropping his briefcase atop May's concrete swan.

"Ms. Schneider?"

Looking now, still with only the end-of-block streetlight for illumination, Jaron saw his mistake. It *was* Ms. Schneider (one of them, anyway), and not a decoration after all. But even after he spoke, the woman didn't move. She had her arms at her sides, head somewhat down, a rat's nest of long gray hair covering her like a shade to a lamp. She said nothing, but that wasn't unusual. Politically incorrect or not, Jaron couldn't help thinking of the Schneider triplets as spinsters.

They were identical and at least seventy, and they seemed to speak no English at all. If spinsters were still a thing, the Schneider sisters were it. They lived in a ramshackle house, just the three of them, and neighborhood kids were afraid to retrieve frisbees tossed into their yard. The house usually smelled like gingerbread. They never sold or gave any away — not to the neighborhood, nor at block-wide bake sales.

What did they do with all that gingerbread? Was it all they ate, like characters from a fairytale?

"Are you okay, Ms. Schneider? Is there anything I can help you with?" Jaron wanted to be more personable, but he couldn't tell which one it was. They were Gerta, Betta, and Inga, and none of them ever spoke to anyone. May said it was cruel to treat them like witches; they were just lonely immigrants who'd never really left the old country.

And they were odd, too — not scary strange like the kids said, but kind of *sad*. Rumor said some drug company had enrolled them in a trial that, though the promises were vague, Jaron somehow interpreted as positive for the neighborhood. He got a sense that if the trial worked, they'd be more social. It was true to Jaron's halfway civility that he never actually asked what the drug did. Maybe it made them less crazy. That would be a step in the right direction.

But if that was its aim, then the drug wasn't working. If Jaron didn't know the woman had a face, he would have doubted it now. With all that ratty hair touching her shoulders, he could only see the Reaper he'd originally imagined. He could hear her rough breath but could only really see her bottom lip, hanging open, black in the nighttime air.

Jaron waved a hand behind him, refusing to move his eyes away from the visitor. He wanted the motion-activated porch light to come on, but it remained stubbornly off.

"Would you like me to call someone for you?" Jaron asked.

Nothing.

"I can walk you home if you'd like."

He really hoped she wouldn't choose now to wake up and get excited. On a list of things Jaron didn't want to do tonight, walking one of the Schneiders three doors down to their gray-boarded house was number two. The only thing above it was peeling the skin off his body.

The figure kept on saying nothing.

"You sure I can't get you anything?" She must have come to his house for a reason, after all.

But still, not a word.

"Well," he said, "goodnight."

Once through the door, Jaron locked it, then turned off the foyer light so he could peep through the glass. He didn't want to take his eyes off the woman outside for a second.

"You're late," said May.

Jaron jumped a foot. She laughed, then seemed just a little worried.

"Jesus. You freaked me out."

"By saying hello?"

"By ..." He looked out again, but the woman was gone. "Never mind."

They moved into the kitchen. Jaron dropped his briefcase on the island. May moved it off with an annoyed expression, same as always, then resumed chopping fat red peppers on a worn wooden board.

Jaron sat on one of the stools around the island. "Have you seen the Schneiders recently?"

May shrugged. "I don't know. Why?"

He looked toward the front door. "One of them was outside."

"Outside?"

"In the driveway."

"Why?"

"I don't know why." He shook his head. "I think they're going senile."

"Which one was it?"

"I don't know. But I don't think it matters. I think they're all going nuts."

"That's a bit ageist, don't you think?"

Jaron didn't think so. "Last week, I walked by,

and they were watering their sidewalk. Two of them, with separate hoses."

May gave a good-natured roll of her eyes. "That's a European thing. They wash the stoop."

"They weren't washing. They were watering. The way you water plants."

May flapped a hand. "Oh, pshaw."

"I'm telling you … I wonder if I should call someone."

"Why, because little old ladies are acting like little old ladies?"

They weren't little. In their prime, the Schneiders had probably topped six feet. They were still as tall as Jaron was now. "What if they have that disease?"

"Which?" She wasn't really listening.

"Rabies."

"How would they get rabies?"

"You know what I mean. Not *rabies* rabies. I mean that other thing."

"What, Rip Daddy?"

"Yeah. What if they have that, and they're just going crazier and crazier?"

"That's really between them and Molly."

"Molly's just Meals on Wheels. She's—"

"She's a nurse, is what she is. I talked to Priya

the other day, and she was saying how Molly's checking in on them now. I think the family may be trying to get them into some sort of eldercare facility."

"Well. That's good."

"Unless you're worried they're going to spread it to the neighborhood."

"Of course not." But yes, that's precisely what Jaron was thinking. Only after May's words did he remember what people said about Rip Daddy. It looked scary and definitely could be, but by all accounts, it wasn't transmissible. Those who got it seemed to rot from the inside, but not even once had any of the sufferers turned violent. Rip Daddy was a tragedy, not a threat.

Jaron knew that, and if he kept pushing this with May, she'd make him feel like a bigot. What had happened outside, if she was right, was like Jaron running scared from someone with any other affliction. Diabetes, autism, heart disease, clinical depression. If he didn't change the subject, she'd start telling him he should be more compassionate. The poor women's problems didn't threaten all those lucky enough to be healthy, happy, and loved by family. The Schneiders, by all accounts, had none of those things outside of their little trio.

"When's dinner?"

"I didn't want to start until I was sure when you'd be back. We've got a bit."

"Want help?"

"Sure. You can empty that."

She pointed at the overflowing trash can.

"That's Len's job," he said.

"Okay. Then go get him."

Jaron took this as the taunt it was intended to be. Len was fourteen now and could only be separated from his video games by the jaws of life or the promise of pizza. Since they were having a pasta medley for dinner and Jaron didn't feel like a fight, it would be easier to do the boy's job for him.

He raised the lid and tugged out the bag, trying to pretend he didn't see the disapproving way May looked at him. It wasn't fair to be seen as spineless by your wife. Not after a hard day's work. Where were his slippers? Where was his beer?

"Don't you think it's important for him to—"

"It's just faster this way," Jaron said.

He took the bag to the rear and tossed it into the alleyway can. The backyard was a mess. Len had also been shirking his lawn mowing duty, and Amber's toys were so covered by the tall grass, he'd have to go spelunking for them before so much as starting the mower. Good luck getting such proactivity from Len, who hadn't even had the initiative to be born on a day that came every year.

Sighing, Jaron looked through his home's lit windows and, by their scant light, began to pick through the grass. He'd retrieved two trainer roller-skates and (of all things) the missing living room remote before turning toward the unsettling sound of something behind him.

Near one side of the short fence between yard and alley was Ms. Schneider again. Jaron startled and moved to head back inside, but his wife's words clanged in his mind. She was a lonely old woman who hadn't been in her right mind for a while. The darkness outside didn't change that.

Jaron steeled himself and moved closer.

"Is it Gerta?"

She didn't respond.

"Inga. You're Inga, right?"

Still nothing. Jaron was wearing a smile he didn't feel, trying to make his voice friendly.

"I guess that just leaves Betta. Is that you, Betta?"

She made a noise, like a groan. As she did, Jaron saw that lower lip again. It was slack, foamed with saliva. A runner dangled like a tiny mountaineer rappelling from her chin.

Rip Daddy. He knew it.

She had the bug, and even though Jaron knew it was harmless unless you managed to get it (and nobody really knew how that happened yet, but it wasn't from proximity or contact), the presence of the disease so close to home freaked him out. There'd been around four hundred cases so far, but most of them had been on the opposite side of town. A few were in other cities (mostly San Diego, San Francisco, and L.A., plus a few all the way on the East Coast), but folks here in Bakersfield had gotten the brunt of it. Why? It wasn't clear. Something in the food, maybe — something sourced locally. Oranges? Grapes? Maybe walnuts. It'd just be spectacular if the latest autumn illness came from a bunch of stupid nuts. And now here was one of the local spinsters, dripping with the infection. It made Jaron feel like his family might be next.

He forced himself to move closer. "Ms. Schneider, are you feeling okay?"

She groaned again. This time her hands twitched.

"When's the last time you've been to a doctor?"

Another groan, but she still hadn't looked up.

"Look. Maybe this isn't my place, but you know about this … this disease, I guess, that's going around? Rip Daddy?"

Nothing. He opened the gate, moved into the narrow alley, and closed it again behind him.

"I know you and your sisters don't go out much to, you know, get exposed, but they don't know how people get it yet. Could be something you ate. You could all be sick if you're sharing the same food."

Her mouth seemed to have changed. A bit of a snarl, pissed at his presumption.

"Look. I just think maybe you should get checked out. I've heard on the news … The symptoms. Supposed to be like …" He was faltering before this unhelpful audience. He pantomimed rubbing drool off his lip. "Saliva. People produce a lot of saliva. And I can't help but notice that you …"

A new noise came from behind him. Jaron startled; he thought she'd just teleported from one end of the alley to the other. But no, it was a second woman. Another of the sisters, dressed and looking exactly the same. Both were in nightgowns that looked torn and dusty, and only now did he notice their feet. Both were bare, and in the wan light, appeared near-black and covered in what seemed to be lesions.

The new woman growled. Jaron eyed one, then the other.

"Oh, good," he said, not feeling good at all. "I guess what I was saying is for all of you. The thing is, Rip Daddy affects the brain." He tapped his head, in case they didn't know what a brain was. Then he remembered that maybe they didn't; nobody had ever heard the Schneiders speak anything other than German, and it was possible they didn't understand anything in English.

"If it's affecting your brain," he said, forgetting all about the differences between English and German, "you can't think right. You do things like … well … like go out in your nightgown without slippers. You might not think to get tested because you're just not … not thinking right, you know?"

They started to walk slowly toward him, closing in from both sides.

"I'll…" He searched for something to do or say — something not cowardly or stupid. He could be noble. No matter what May said. "I'll call someone for you. Sound good?"

Now they both groaned, still advancing.

He saw mouths open. Their teeth were covered with something black, like tar.

"Maybe I could drive you to urgent care." This, he didn't remotely mean. If he was driving these two spooks anywhere, they'd be in a locked trailer far behind his vehicle. "What do you say? Feel better in the morning?"

Another lie, of course. Rip Daddy didn't have a cure and was fatal within days.

This is your brain; this is your brain on Rip Daddy; this is your brain after it's been sugared and whipped into hard peaks of meringue.

He'd be taking them to medical custody where the two of them could die, but at least they wouldn't be prowling the shadows like alley cats.

They were right on him now. Six feet away at most. Even knowing he couldn't catch it, Jaron felt a paranoid urge to keep away. He should let it all go. Call the police if he had to instead of yelling for help; let May come out here to nursemaid them if she found that weak-willed.

He had his hand on the gate before he knew it, preparing to step through and leave them out here to spit and hiss. He hoped they wouldn't die behind his house. Rumor said brain leaked through Rip Daddy ears when it was over, and the resulting goo was impossible to scrub from wood or concrete.

"Okay. Have a nice evening, the—"

He was staring at the third sister, this one inside his yard on the other side of the fence. Instead of turning to walk inside, he turned right into her face.

There was a knife buried to its hilt in her throat. Her front was an apron of dried blood. Jaron didn't know much about anatomy, but he did know that the blade looked to be three inches wide at its broadest point, and its sideways position pretty much had to have severed her esophagus, windpipe, and probably one or both of the big arteries.

But still, the woman was upright. She was breathing, but it was a strange kind of breath. Passive more than active, the way you breathe for someone in CPR. A small flap beneath the knife blade opened and closed to reveal a pure black interior.

"Jesus," he said, fighting a panic-blinding surety that with that wound, she should be dead — she absolutely *had* to be dead. "You need to get to—!"

Jaron never said the rest.

Unlike the Schneider sisters, he found himself unable to breathe once his neck was ripped to jerky.

TWO

Routine and Urgent

Thom Shelton wouldn't stop checking the news.

That was his engineer's nature. He wanted to codify, label, name, and ultimately understand everything there was to be understood. Carly kept telling him that not everything could be explained, but Thom always thought her words were more spiritual than practical. She thought that everything happened for a reason (it didn't), that everyone had a purpose (they didn't) and that somewhere deep down, fathers always loved their sons — which was relevant today more than most days, but no less bullshit.

So when she chastised Thom by telling him that he'd never understand all that happened, it was an easy thing to brush away. Carly might as well be telling him that his aura's colors were off, or that he shouldn't conduct any banking while Mercury was still in retrograde.

After saying it twice, however, she wrapped her smooth hands with their purple fingernails around his phone, delicately removed it from his grip, then dropped it into her purse.

"Excuse me?" Thom asked.

"Nobody knows, Thom. Get it? *Nobody knows.*"

"Nobody's trying very hard, then."

She looked for Brendan before speaking. He was fourteen and plenty capable of hearing his parents discuss an illness he was too immortal to ever get, but that right there was half the problem — and this, Thom understood far better than his wife. Carly was the go-with-the-flow, let's-be-honest-instead-of-protecting-him-from-every-little-thing parent, and by default that turned Thom into the bad guy. He didn't love that role, but the alternative was to give in and treat Brendan like the adult he hadn't yet become.

That's what Thom's father had done, but how had that turned out? Rick spent more time jumping from airplanes and wandering the earth even after Thom was born than he spent parenting, and whenever Thom had tried to confront him about it, Rick's defense was, "You weren't as fragile as you think you were."

These days Carly and Rick said the same sorts of things about Brendan, and it wasn't true; Thom refused to *let* it be true. He didn't want his son fragile, but he didn't want him foolhardy like his grandfather, either. If Carly hadn't looked to be sure Brendan wasn't around before speaking now, Thom would have been. At least she was learning to respect his wishes that much.

"Diseases come up and go away in nature," Carly told Thom, quieter.

They weren't to the front desk of Shady Acres yet, and he needed to finish this conversation before they did. The clerks weren't health workers, but they worked with all the eldercare folks here and would, in all likelihood, fancy themselves experts. Thom wanted to hear from realists, not experts.

There was a disease out there and its reports were getting stranger all the time. It wasn't that Thom wanted its threat eradicated so much as he wanted a reasonable answer already. Every time there was a new flu, the CDC knew exactly where it came from. Rip Daddy had the CDC scratching their heads, and instead it was the bio nerds at Hemisphere advancing most of the theories.

How was Rip Daddy outsmarting the CDC? *It wasn't.* Thom was sure there had to be more to the story.

"Are you listening to me?"

"Of course I am." Thom reached out, took back his phone.

"Are you sure? Because if I had to guess, I'd say you're just being a big old bitch."

"What?" Thom asked.

"You heard me. I love you, Thomas, and I know you're a strong-willed man with an amazing head on your shoulders."

"Thank you."

"But I also know that when it comes to your father, all that intelligence flies right out the window. Instead, you become a whiny bitch. Remember Carl Treeger?"

"Carly, I—"

"Whenever you're around Rick, you're a bigger bitch than Carl Treeger."

"You know you're a woman, right?"

"Oh, this has nothing to do with gender. The kind of bitch you get around Rick, it's like new words have to be made before we can properly define how bitchy you are. It's unreal."

"Carly, this is—"

She took his phone back, delicate but firm. "Then prove me wrong. You weren't this interested in the news at home and you weren't interested in the car. You only got obsessed with epidemiology once we got within sight of the front desk. Now. Look. You know he's doing much better. The caretakers say he's lucid way more often than not. Nobody wants to say that it's working, but I'll say it; *I think it's working*. And I'd know, since I see your father way more often than you do. Now tell me. Is that what an intelligent, stand-up person should be able to say about his father — that his spouse pays more attention than he does? Or is that what a bitch would say?"

"Carly …"

"Say my name all you want. But do it *after* you sign us in. You can talk on the way. Maybe see what Brendan thinks."

Low blow and checkmate. Thom was forcibly reminded that despite his many degrees and accolades, his half-hippie wife was far smarter than he was. He couldn't obsess and fret in a group because if he did it around Brendan, the boy would become cavalier and start looking for loopholes to poke through his father's outbreak rules … and if he did it around Rick, the old man would then humiliate Thom badly enough to send him on his way clucking back home with his tail tucked neatly between his legs.

The only place *to* procrastinate and pout was right here and now, shy of the front desk with only Carly in earshot. Closing that door would leave Thom with no choice but to fall into line.

"Fine," he said.

She handed him the phone and he put it into his pocket, making a mental note to codify the news stories later. It probably wouldn't happen; Carly was annoyingly correct that he was only truly interested when it could keep him from having to visit his father. It was like what his mom, when she'd been alive, had called "bus-itis" — a sickness the kids woke up with, then recovered from the minute the school bus had passed them by.

They went to the desk and Thom, to save his dignity, signed the three of them in to visit one Richard Shelton, Room 720. The girl behind the desk was wearing dinosaur scrubs and smiled at Carly. Do-gooder. Carly didn't just visit her father-in-law more often than Thom; she also volunteered all over the community with many of the other seniors — mostly early-stage Alzheimer's patients like Rick.

Every once in a while, when Carly got righteous about it (in Thom's opinion, anyway), he considered rebutting with some form of "It must be nice" or "Sure, it's easy when." But in truth it wasn't easy for Carly to volunteer at Shady Acres. She fit a half hour of reading-to-the-elderly in during three lunch breaks per week, and her hospital was six traffic-packed miles away.

Often, after a full day of anesthetizing patients followed by a delicious family dinner, Carly went back to volunteer in the evenings. Thom usually said he was too tired to join her and she pretended to accept his excuse as something close to valid. Once she was gone, he tried to forget that he worked behind a desk and she was on her feet most of the day. Stupid damn Woman of the Year.

To Carly's credit, she lorded none of this over Thom unless he forced her to, like he had out front. If he accepted a family visit to Rick once a month without complaining about it, he could go long stretches of time in which she let him pretend he was some sort of antiquated Man of the House when, in fact, he was nothing of the sort.

It was a delicate mental balancing act, wherein Thom was both protector and antagonist. He was the one who swore he was doing nothing wrong but he was also his own accuser. Trying to hide from your own insults almost required a pair of separate personalities. Thom, who was of two minds about his father already, did his very best.

They found Rick on the seventh floor polishing knives.

"Christ, Dad," said Thom, rushing in to take them. "Do they know you have these?"

"They're mine." Rick wasn't perturbed even though Thom had just taken his toys. His expression read as it always did. *I'll get my way in the end, and if you don't believe it, then you can just try and stop me.*

"You're not allowed to have weapons."

"They're not weapons, Tommy. They're knives."

"Knives are weapons."

And Brendan, taking two of the knives from a side table upon which Thom had sat them, said, "Cool! Where did you get these, Grandpa?"

"Monster hunters," Rick said.

"Dad …"

"*Really*, Grandpa."

"I'm serious! Did you watch *An American Werewolf in London* like I told you?"

Brendan laughed. "What about *The Shining*?"

"There's no monsters in *The Shining*," said Carly.

"Oh. That's where you're wrong. 'This inhuman place makes human monsters.'"

"He's too young for those movies," Thom said. "Stop baiting him, Dad."

"He's fourteen."

"Exactly: He's fourteen!"

"Only seems younger because you baby him like your mother babied you."

"*OOOOKAY*," Carly said, cutting a diagonal swath through the room, between Thom on one side and Rick and Brendan on the other. It was just one word, but she'd honed it to a perfect edge as an all-purpose peace bludgeon. She'd taught herself to smile a little while saying it and to pitch her tone just so, thereby somehow conveying mild annoyance *(That's just about enough of that, you two, and I mean it!)* and amusement *(Oh, you silly boys and your ways.)* in unison. It was neither too rough, which would have raised both men's defenses, nor too amused, which would have encouraged Rick to keep going if only to irritate his buzz-kill son. "Let's get you packed up to go."

"Where am I going?" Rick asked.

"The mall, Dad. We talked about going to the mall, remember?"

Rick's mental state slid on a spectrum between "lucid, socially aggressive, prank-loving ex-Marine" and "paranoid, socially aggressive, mentally confused ex-Marine." Somewhere in the middle, a sweet spot sometimes created "confused and slightly desperate old man," but that one was rare and hadn't shown his face since they'd started Rick on his so-far-so-good pharma trial.

Worse, Rick was aware of them, even when the Alzheimer's had its little flares. Normal Rick (the lucid one) hated the other versions of himself and seemed to have declared war on them all. Guessing his current state and getting it wrong was never a pleasant way to begin.

As Thom realized he'd just done — quite by accident this time.

"I know we talked about the mall, goddammit," Rick snapped, his voice even but full of barbs. "I'm not feeble. But she said 'pack.' Do I need a winter coat and rations? Maybe some MREs?"

"I just meant your wallet and coat."

"And your—" Thom began, but Carly held up a hand where Rick couldn't see.

"And here they are," Carly said instead, going for the wallet on the table.

Technically, yes, Rick required a few more items whenever he was leaving these days. He almost never needed his cane, but Thom always wanted to take it anyway — in case his father spontaneously injured himself like had happened only once four years ago. The cane folded small enough to fit in a bag, so Carly always took the bag along with a light sweater.

With two bag-sized items already in the mix, Carly usually added a bottle of water (Rick complained whenever anyone charged for water) and a small bag of jerky. Rick wasn't supposed to have jerky, but he said most normal snacks were for children or pussies. He wasn't really supposed to eat jerky, but it was easier to just let him have it when so much else was out of routine.

Someone arrived at the door, mid-sentence. A nurse, his head down over a clipboard. Only after reading a bit then finally looking up did he see Rick's small room at capacity.

"Morning, Mr. Shelton! Doc Gellert asked me to come by and ask when you wouldn't mind me poking you again, just one vial this time, and I promise I'll be … Oh, hello! Visitors, I see!"

Carly said hello, then bustled the nurse out of the room. She was always pulling things like this. Privileges of being here so often, volunteering, getting to know the staff. Thom was torn. Everything Carly took off their collective plate was a relief, but he hated that he couldn't handle any of them. A catch-22. In order to deal with his father better, he'd need to spend more time dealing with his father. The math was bizarre. Maybe it wasn't kind, but he'd grown up thinking of nursing homes as set-it-and-forget-it.

Carly returned alone.

"What'd he want?" Rick asked.

"Just some tests. They'll handle it when we get back."

"What tests? I just had all my tests."

"He says one of your proteins tested high."

"Well, in that case, I guess it's time to end it." Rick took one of the knives Thom had confiscated and, before Thom could stop him, put on a gory-hilarious show for his grandson: first faux-slitting his own throat, then faux-committing hari-kari by jamming the blade into his armpit and pretending to strike his gut.

Brendan laughed, and Thom was again conflicted, back to wondering when he'd become so wishy-washy that he couldn't decide whether he preferred Brendan happy here and respecting his elders (he liked Rick's stories but usually hated these visits, said it smelled like stale bread and medicine) or if he should be annoyed that once again, Rick was undermining him with all these unacceptable behaviors: owning and using death knives, rolling around on the floor as his doctors had told him not to do, modeling violence for a kid Thom had tried to keep as much violence from as possible.

Ultimately he didn't need to decide, because Carly went on talking and Rick stopped clowning long enough to listen. As she spoke, Thom watched his father, seeing focus in the old man's eyes. He really was improving. He owed Hemisphere a thank-you for that. If Rick got better and stayed better, maybe he could live on his own for another decade or two and make these visits unnecessary. He was only sixty-eight. His own father, well past ninety, was still alive, still tending a garden and chickens more or less on his own.

"Gregor said it's routine. He can do the test later."

But Thom didn't like what he saw behind

Carly's smiling eyes. Rick and his daughter-in-law got along, but only Thom could read nuance in his wife like he was seeing now.

While Rick gathered his things, Thom pulled her to one side.

"What's going on?" he asked.

"One of your dad's tests came back abnormal," she told him.

"Abnormal how?"

"He didn't say."

"Didn't, or wouldn't? Did you ask?"

That riled her a bit. Her words sharpened and she looked more directly at Thom, no longer casual and to the side. "Yes, I *asked*, Thom. I always ask. All he'd say was that it's an Alzheimer's marker. Something to do with the plaques his medication is supposed to help his brain build new paths around."

"So 'abnormal' means ..."

"He said it's no big deal. Just routine."

Thom shrugged. "Well, then."

"But I took a glance at the paperwork on his clipboard. The order was marked urgent. How can something be routine and urgent at the same time?"

Thom had no answer.

THREE

Like a Sledgehammer

Thom didn't know that Rick's girlfriend's name was Rosie. Largely because he hadn't known his father had a girlfriend.

The very idea was hard to mentally slot. Rick had held three categories for women Thom's entire life, and Rosie's presence seemed to fit none of them.

The first and broadest of Rick's categories was for women with whom there was no attraction — and for an older guy (and a testosterone-fueled one, at that) Rick's attitude towards that rather large group was pleasantly enlightened. Rick, unlike most of his jarhead buddies, might even be called a feminist — but don't ever call him one to his face; Thom had seen that lesson learned the hard way.

The second category was for unentangled recreational sex, of which Rick had in abundance after Thom's mother died — and, per Rick's stories, which he'd had a copious amount of (and in many ports around the world) before they'd met.

The third category was for that rare woman with whom Rick could actually be kind, tender, and downright romantic … but in a sensible world there was only one woman in that group, and her name had been Marie Shelton, *nee* Watts. With her death, that phase of Rick's life should have ended. Mom had been his one category-three shot, and that was all there was to it.

Seeing Rick exhibit third-category behavior with this new woman was bizarre more than bothersome. Thom wasn't truly upset. He just didn't understand. It was even stranger given that the woman in question was sixty-six years old — an age Thom's middle-aged brain had yet to equate with … you know … still wanting to be alive and social.

Thom wasn't yet forty; he'd decided in what he suspected was probably an ageist way that white-haired ladies knitted; they didn't date. He'd discussed this theory with Carly. Once. She'd scowled, then asked Thom how he was planning to feel in twenty-five years when *they* were near retirement age, and Thom had thought she was changing the subject.

Only after he was sleeping on the couch that night did he realize what her question really meant. He shouldn't have answered, "achy when it rains," and "excited about the early bird buffet," both of which had earned him scathing looks.

He probably should have lied. Said he was mature enough to see more than skin deep.

"Rosie can't go with us," Carly explained.

Rick gave a well-reasoned argument he'd clearly been formulating for a while: "Bullshit."

"She's not our relative. We can't sign her out."

Thom, uncomfortable with this new tension between his wife and his father, found himself out of the fray and hence just a foot from the non-relative in question. She asked him what he did for a living. Distracted, he gave Rosie his wife's profession.

"You're good to your father," Rosie said.

Oh, sweet Rosie. She hadn't met Thom, apparently.

"Thanks."

"Where are we going, did you say?"

Carly, hearing this, reached out to put her hand on the woman's wrist. "I'm sorry, Rosie. We aren't going anywhere. Another time, okay?" Then she immediately turned back to Rick. "*No.* And I mean it; do you hear me?"

Her firm voice, which she almost never used with Rick. An excellent sign; Carly's firm voice was like a caveman's club, and she didn't wield it against those who were too weak for its blows. The fact that she was speaking to Rick more like an opponent than a dependent meant she must see the mental changes as much Thom did.

Rick wasn't fully back to his old, decade-past self; he dipped in and out of temporary dementia with shocking ease and had, just since they'd left the room, made two references to being stalked by monsters that neither Thom nor Carly thought were for Brendan's amusement. Even the boy had looked at his mother when Rick said the second thing, about being followed and the need to watch the shadows. But now — and a lot more often, lately — Rick was rock solid.

Rosie turned to Thom again. "Are we going to the movies?"

Thom shook his head. "The mall."

He'd already told her twice. He'd also told her his name two times and confirmed, just once, that he was not Rosie's own son. Her forgetfulness was undermining Thom's confidence that if Rick won this custody debate (he would), Rosie would be a casual ride-along. Her mental decay seemed mild enough to be more amusing than alarming, but still she had an illness, and that made Thom plenty nervous.

The war at the checkout desk continued until Carly made two fatal mistakes. First, she let Rick sneak in that it was Rosie's birthday tomorrow and that he'd promised her a night (or at least a day) on the town to celebrate — something a girl named Floris (seriously) at the desk confirmed.

Floris, Thom gathered from context, was actually Rosie's daughter ... and that was Carly's second mistake. Carly said, in front of Floris and Rick, that rules were rules, that nobody could sign out a resident they weren't authorized to sign out. She delivered this missive with a palm-brushing finality, as conclusive as writing *QED* at the end of a logic problem.

But Thom knew what would happen next, and sure enough it went one-two-three.

Rick turned on the charm for Floris, who he'd clearly been bewitching since moving into the place, and Floris said she'd be happy to sign her mother into the Sheltons' custody if it was okay with Carly.

All eyes turned to Carly, then suddenly there she was, hoisted by her own petard. She'd have to be irresponsible and let Rosie come or be the bad guy. Given Thom's avoidant personality, that was her usual role so often already.

Five minutes later they were all in Thom's minivan, with him behind the wheel like a beleaguered dad on a vacation he hadn't asked to take and actively didn't want to go on. He kept his eyes forward, forcing all conversational balls through Carly because this was all her fault; she'd allowed this to happen. Now, in addition to an afternoon spent with his father mocking his life choices and suggesting he was a wimp for not serving in the military or having any real adventures, he had to spend it with another senior on his conscience.

Although, maybe it'd be okay. Maybe Rosie's presence would occupy Rick so much that he wouldn't have time to suggest that real men used guns and shovels instead of calculators and pens. More time with Rosie meant less time telling Thom to "live a little, for Christ's sake" and suggesting he allow his son to do the same.

Brendan, though he hated Shady Acres, was otherwise the second pea in his grandfather's pod. Thom had nightmares in which Brendan became

Rick. He didn't just model all of his grandfather's destructive behaviors (which he already did in more ways than Thom wanted to count); he actually turned sixty-eight and got liver spots on his arms. It'd been terrible, a nightmare that followed him into the day.

"You hear about that thing in Rosedale?" came Rick's voice from the rear.

There was really no way not to have, unless you avoided the news entirely. "Not now, Dad."

"Oh. I get it. You're afraid your kid can't take it."

"I can take it!" Brendan said. "What is it, Grandpa?"

"I said no, Brendan."

"Some guy was eaten alive," Rick said.

Rosie gasped. "Oh my."

"Ate him like a steak."

"Gross!" said Brendan with elation.

"Dammit, Dad."

"Please. You raise him like a marshmallow, he'll think he's living in chocolate. What happens when he gets drafted?"

"There's no draft anymore," said Carly.

"What about Vietnam?"

Thom and Carly traded a glance.

"Vietnam is over, Rick."

"*You* didn't even fight in Vietnam, Dad," Thom added.

"I know what I fought in! I didn't even mean the Vietnam War!"

Rick probably expected them to ask, *What about Vietnam, then?*, but Thom wasn't about to bite.

When Rick got frazzled or excited, he tended to use representative avatars for the things he meant rather than the correct things themselves. Apparently "Vietnam," in Rick's mind, was the conflict everyone understood for a grizzled vet, even though it'd been well before his time.

But Rick also remembered working on a farm (he hadn't, but strong boys did inside his mind) and, most troublingly, had started to misremember his time with Thom's mother. Sometimes he alluded to a 1950s-style marriage in which Marie had been waiting for him in high heels and a flowered apron when he came home, dinner already on the table with the brandy and cigars set out for after. But Marie had been a dental hygienist and had, at the time, worked longer hours than Rick. Thom had eaten most of his childhood meals in front of the TV while his father drank beer from a tall pilsner glass, perfectly centered on the coaster beneath it.

"There's something living in my closet," Rick said out of the blue.

"Really?" Brendan asked. "What?"

"I can't see what it looks like. The thing always hides when I open the door."

"Cool!"

"There's nothing in your closet," Thom said without turning.

And to think, he'd recently been wondering if Rick might be well enough to move back out on his own. He hated entertaining his father's fantasies. They made him feel unseated. Good dads were supposed to deny the presence of closet monsters, not propose them.

"Of course *you'd* say that," Rick answered.

"I believe you," said Rosie.

Rick nodded emphatically. "I'm not talking about the boogeyman. This is a real thing."

"Sure it is."

Rick spoke so rationally about his delusions and became so angry when they were questioned, sometimes Thom wondered if somehow, some way, there really was a monster in there.

"Goddammit, I'm not senile! You think I'm senile, don't you?"

The answer was … yes, clearly, by medical diagnosis, undeniably and without question.

Thom was spared having to deliver an answer when Brendan changed the topic. He'd pulled his phone from his pocket, and already Carly was reaching to confiscate it.

"Oh, wow! Grandpa Rick was right — it says someone stripped this guy's arm all the way to the *bone!*"

Brendan made the announcement with the sort of glee usually reserved for rollercoaster rides. Thom, who'd seen gonzo footage on the news, felt differently. Bakersfield had been getting weirder and weirder over the past few weeks. Thom wasn't so sure it was his imagination. He'd heard of a few more murders than usual and kept seeing people — mostly older folks — behaving in ways that seemed *off*, like an under-the-skin surrealist painting.

Now this — murder by cannibal? What Brendan hadn't said yet (and, hopefully, he hadn't yet learned from whatever news site he was reading) was that the poor man's head had also been smashed by something very large. Like a sledgehammer.

"That's enough of that," Carly said, grasping

while her son held his phone out of reach. "Give it to me, Brendan."

He relented.

"One of my friends got caught up in that," Rosie said.

"What?" Carly turned to look back.

"Well, I guess not a friend so much as an acquaintance. One of the ladies in that story used to come into the drug shop when I worked there."

"What ladies?"

"And when?" Thom added.

"Oh, I don't know," said Rosie in an airy way that made Thom wonder if he should take what came next seriously or dismiss it out of hand. "You know. The Walgreens."

"Walgreens?" Rick said.

"What?" Carly asked him.

"That was last year. She only worked at a Walgreens for a while before …" He trailed off, but they all knew what he meant. Rosie had once been a pharmacist, but they'd let her work the counter, with no drug privileges, once she'd started getting forgetful. Eventually there'd been no way to keep her on, but by then Rosie didn't seem to mind at all.

"Okay," said Thom, withdrawing his attention from the big bag of nothing.

"I think her name was Inga."

Thom's mouth fell from an amused smile to something more sour. There'd been an Inga in the news story. He was sure of it; he'd had a horrible aunt by that name.

"Inga Smith," Rosie said.

"*Schneider*," Brendan corrected. He'd gotten his phone back when Rosie had provided her distraction and was now reading all the things Thom had hoped he wouldn't.

"That's right," said Rosie. "Inga Schneider. She and her sisters went to First Methodist on Eighth. No, Seventh."

Thom tried to ignore her and keep his eyes on the road.

Before her death, Rick's mother had been a lot like Rosie was now. She couldn't remember Thom's children between visits because they'd been born after her mind started to change, but she'd never lost track of obscure facts from long ago, like the exact shoes she'd worn to her cousin's wedding. Rosie had that confidence in her voice now, and Inga Schneider was indeed the name he'd heard. The dead (eaten) man was named Jason something ... No, no; it was *Jaron* ... but three neighborhood women had gone missing at the same time. Sisters. Triplets, all identical, reclusive and strange.

"They're spreading." Rick sounded emphatic. "I just know it. I can hear the monsters multiplying in my head."

"Okay," said Carly.

"Don't patronize me."

"I'm not patronizing you."

"Me either, Dad." Thom was somewhere between frightened and annoyed. "In fact, I'm not even listening."

"Thomas!" Carly hissed.

Thom shot her a stare. "What, am I supposed to just go along with this? He's scaring Brendan."

"Grandpa's not scaring me, Dad."

"It's always like this," Thom went on, realizing he was about to speak about Rick as if he weren't present and far beyond caring. "He's got a built-in excuse no matter what he says. If he's making sense, then he's my father and I should respect him. If he's calling women 'broads' and pinching their asses—"

"I don't do that anymore!"

"—then he's just a harmless old man who grew up in a different day and age. If he's racist—"

"I'm not racist!"

"Really? So you're okay with Mexicans 'taking our jobs'?"

"That's not racist; it's—"

"And when he's acting batshit crazy, sorry Brendan, he can't help himself! When does he have to accept responsibility for his own actions? *When?*"

"How about when I was storming beaches with an M4 in my hands while you were still shitting in your diaper?" Rick said.

Brendan laughed, then squelched it immediately.

"Okay. Fine, Dad. Keep pulling out that old chestnut. It definitely forgives everything else. It's like you did confession in advance, right?"

"I did a lot of things in advance. That's what men do, Thomas. They *do things.*"

"So now you're insulting Carly?"

"Don't bring me into this." She already had sufficient frost in her voice to promise a week's worth of cold shoulder.

"I'm using 'men' as a general term. Carly's more man than you are."

She turned on him. "I don't need your help either, Rick!"

"Insulting," Thom said. "The only perspective that matters is yours, same as it's always been."

"I'm sorry I'm hurting your feelings while taking care of you and providing for you all of your life. I was taught by my old man that a father's job isn't to be his kids' friend, but their *father*."

"You can be both. Brendan and I are friends. Maybe we won't hate each other like …" *Too far.* "Maybe things will be different for us. Right, Brendan?"

Brendan was playing a game on the phone. From what Thom saw when he turned his head, the kid had stopped listening.

"Enough," Carly tried.

"We come out here," Thom said, "we spend our time and our money to pick you up for a fun day …"

"Hey. No sweat off my balls. You're bored with this, take us back." Rick grunted.

"It's nice to be out with family," Rosie said, sounding oblivious.

The van's tires hummed on the road. The only other sound was the quiet tapping of Brendan's finger on his phone's screen.

"Turn right here," Rick said after the quiet had continued too long. "Quickly. We're being followed."

FOUR

Good For You, Son

THE PARLIAMENT MALL had found a temporary solution to its enormous empty anchor space — a JCPenney that went out of business and left a gaping hole in the mall's bottom line. Thom, who saw the mall as a default neutral space to take his father on these excursions — one that was lively and distracting enough that nobody felt obligated to carry on a conversation — had been worrying about that gaping hole since the JCPenney had its fire sale and moved the hell out of Bakersfield.

Anchor stores provided most of a mall's rent. Without something in the entire east corner, Thom felt sure the place would go bankrupt and close. There were no other nearby malls. They'd have to go out to lunch or something, and then how would he manage to avoid conversation?

But the mall's empty gullet was now filled with a holiday store. Crammed with Halloween decorations now, but Thom could see a few animatronic Santas and over-the-top nativities edging forward from the rear, suggesting that the Christmas store would be coming soon. Good. The place would survive a little longer.

Unfortunately, Thom found himself unable to enjoy the relief at seeing its vacancy filled. He was too annoyed from the drive, and still pumped with adrenaline from the last five minutes. Rick's certainty that they were being followed (and that there were creatures lurking in doorways) had grown from ridiculous to, with Brendan's help, almost credible.

After several minutes of Rick insisting he kept seeing the same cars behind him, Thom said that's how it worked; cars tended to follow each other long distances when traveling on main routes. But Brendan was sure he'd seen the same blue Kia well before they got onto 58. It also had a dent on its fender.

Thom said it was coincidence.

Rosie said she thought two other cars looked familiar.

Thom tried to say Rosie didn't really know what she'd seen but by then Carly was in the fray, playing caretaker but doing more harm than good. In a semantic fight (or perhaps an attempt to help Rosie improve her memory), Carly asked Rosie which cars she remembered for sure, just to test her mind and see if there was anything to it, but then Rick heard her and became even more agitated.

Brendan started spotting cars that sort of matched Rosie's descriptions, arguing with his father that Grandpa might be right. Rick's commands increased in volume, and it all must have sounded reasonable to Brendan because he grew more animated and louder too. Thom was pretty sure the only thing his dad was doing with those shouts was quoting lines from movie chase scenes his father had always enjoyed.

The French Connection, Dirty Harry, The Dark Knight.

At one point Rick said they had a hundred miles to the mall, that they had a full tank of gas and half a pack of cigarettes, it's dark out, and they were wearing sunglasses.

This confused Brendan, but Thom just said, "It's *106* miles. To *Chicago*." Nobody appreciated his trivia skills, hearing Rick's words as real observations instead of lines from *The Blues Brothers*.

The situation kept rotting, and somehow Thom found himself zigzagging between lanes and turning on a moment's notice to elude their imaginary pursuers. When they reached the mall, he was both angry and humiliated. Angry because Rick had riled everyone up again and humiliated because somehow he'd let himself get caught up in it.

Couldn't he just have kept saying no, no matter how much Brendan told him to just listen, Grandpa's right?

Couldn't he have kept his own compass, instead of falling right into his father's weird vortex all over again?

"Let's just sit a while," Thom said.

"We sat the whole way here. I thought I was supposed to be the old man."

Thom sat in an outer ring of the food court anyway, not caring if they all just walked away. "Are those people still after us, Dad?"

"Of course not. Now they're planning."

A sigh. "Planning what?"

"Do you remember Miles?"

"Miles?" Thom repeated.

"Miles Pope, from the trials?"

"I don't know everyone in your drug trial, Dad. Not something that's really on my radar."

"Miles understands."

"Oh? Does 'Miles' live at the Acres?"

But Thom knew perfectly well that he didn't. Rick's capacity at the trial's start had been rocky at best — far worse than now, Thom had just realized — so Thom and Carly had received all the disclosures and signed all the consent forms on his father's behalf. Thom specifically remembered the Hemisphere rep explaining that there were only two test subjects per county. Some weird precaution the company was taking that Thom hadn't cared enough to understand.

Thom was clear on the one thing that mattered: if Rick was the only subject in his retirement home (the other was ten miles away, in Wharton Gardens), at least they wouldn't end up in a *Cocoon* scenario wherein the old men ran around rejuvenated and irresponsible together, talking about their vigorous erections. Rick did enough damage on his own, with just the one dick.

So whoever this Pope was, he couldn't be a friend. Just another delusion, probably. Thom didn't chase the topic. Yet another subject it was hard to start caring about.

Surprising Thom, Rick sat opposite him. He crossed his well-muscled arms (they'd never quite deflated), replete with fading blue-black tattoos. His crystal blue eyes fixed his son's for long enough to show Thom just how lucid he was.

"You think I'm having an episode. Think I'm losing my marbles, is that right?"

"No," Thom muttered, instantly cowed.

Rick looked up at Carly, wordlessly giving instructions. Hearing it, she suddenly became interested in an information kiosk, to which she dragged Rosie and Brendan, out of earshot.

"Tell the truth," Rick said.

"You have Alzheimer's. It would be irresponsible for me not to take what you say with a grain of salt, especially when it's …"

(Batshit crazy.)

"… outside of my experience."

"I'm better now."

"You're better sometimes. Not all the time."

"You didn't see my CAT scan. They did that and an MRI. They said they could see new pathways forming."

"Uh-huh."

"You don't believe me?"

Not really.

Rick said he had a monster in his closet, that they were being followed, that he could hear the minds of people he'd met once in a random drug trial, and he'd spent the drive shouting movie lines he thought he was inventing himself. It didn't matter how clear and cogent he sometimes seemed (*most* times, really, including now); there was no question that Rick's facts were melting into his fantasies.

Thom had heard of no brain scans, and he was supposed to be Rick's medical contact.

"That drug they're giving me? *It's working*, Thomas. You don't like what I'm saying so you're dismissing it, but I'm not making this up."

"It's not a matter of 'making it up,' Dad. You have a *biological condition.* Nobody's blaming you for—"

"It's doing more for me than helping me to stop forgetting and imagining things. And by the way, it's not just me saying that. The Hemisphere folks told me this might happen — that I might develop 'beneficial cerebral side effects.'"

"When? When did they tell you this?"

"Many times. Over and over."

"I see."

"They did!"

"Okay. Okay, Dad. You win. People are following you. You're special. Monsters, telepathy — I'm all in." For some reason, Thom's mind flashed on the "urgent but routine" test the nurse had wanted before they'd left.

One of your dad's tests came back abnormal.

But that didn't matter right now, did it?

This was about peace, not being right.

"Now we're here. We lost the cars that were chasing us. So what do you want to do, huh?"

Rick knew he was being patronized, but the best this particular father and son had ever done in life was to reach an impasse. If they weren't actively fighting — if Rick wasn't calling Thom weak and Thom wasn't calling Rick a bully — that meant they were doing well.

Both men glanced at the two women and the boy standing by the kiosk, then gave each other something on the spectrum of a nod. *Let's just let it go,* that look said, *and fight about it tomorrow.*

"I want to take Rosie on the date I promised her," Rick said.

"That's what we're doing right now."

"I told her I'd take her to get frozen yogurt. Days ago. She's all excited."

Thom throttled his irritation. He'd invited Rosie

along on this trip even though he knew Thom wouldn't want her to go? Really?

"Fine. I guess we can get yogurt."

"I don't mean all of us. I mean just me and Rosie."

Thom wondered if he was misunderstanding. "*Just you?* Are you serious?"

"Did you invite me and your mother when you went on dates? I mean, if you ever had any?"

Thom avoided the insult. It was too easy. "You think we'll cramp your style?"

"I'm almost seventy, kid. You don't need to chaperone me."

"See," Thom said, "that's what I can't get you to understand no matter how many times I try. We have to *sign you out,* Dad. I'm sorry that makes you feel like a library book, but that's how it is. Signing you out makes you my responsibility whether you like it or not."

"Dammit, I'm—"

Thom had anticipated the interruption. He steamrolled on, raising his voice over Rick's.

"*But if you thought I'd just neglect all of that for you*, okay." His volume dropped as Rick let him win. Pressing his oh-so-rare authority, Thom then thrust a two-finger gun at Rosie — a gesture that was far cooler and more confident than Thom had ever truly felt in his life.

"Rosie, on the other hand? No way. *No way,* Dad. Think I haven't seen Silver Alerts thrown up on the highway message system? This is how they happen. Frankly, I don't give a shit what you say about me; under no circumstances are you taking her anywhere alone, out of my sight, when I promised her daughter I'd keep her safe. If you want to take your girlfriend for yogurt so bad, then you can do it with the rest of us. Family treat; we *all* go or *none* of us go. I'm hungry for yogurt too. So just try and stop me."

He lowered the fingers, which he'd dared to move toward Rick as his rant rolled on. For a quiet ten seconds, he felt pride like nothing in recent memory. He wasn't a mild engineer right now. He was Rambo. He was The Terminator. He was Cool Hand Luke and James Dean and Henry Hill. Even Rick kept his mouth shut during those seconds. Probably not because he felt Thom was right or even because he respected Thom's principles, but because his son finally got the balls to stand up for himself for a change. *Good for you, son.*

Then Thom's balls were snipped and fell to the floor.

"I think we can swing it."

He looked up to see Carly laying one hand on his shoulder and another on Rick's. She thought she was helping, but really this was more emasculation. Before she'd spoken, Thom had been preparing to administer a conversational Fatality on his father. He could practically hear the crowd yelling, *FINISH HIM!*

Rick's lips betrayed a tiny smile: just for Thom, not for Carly.

"What?" Thom said, though he'd heard just fine.

"Your father wants some privacy. That's fair. I think we can find a way to create the *feeling* of alone."

"But—"

"Brendan's being jerky anyway." She pointed, and Thom saw his son already halfway through the crowd to the atrium. "He said he wants to look at some video games, and I don't think any of us have any interest in doing that." She turned to Rick. "Thom's right. We can't just let you go off alone. Not if Rosie's here. We made a promise."

"I actually just told him that," Thom said.

"But what I *can* do is give you some space. Thom, you can do whatever; just text me when you're ready to go or I'll text you. Rick, go ahead and get yogurt with Rosie." She pointed through a wide-open space. "I'll sit by the fountain and make sure nobody runs anywhere they shouldn't."

"Thank you, Carly." The solution should still feel humiliating for Rick, but right now thumbing his nose at Thom mattered more. He glanced at his son, then moved to stand beside his girlfriend.

Thom looked up at Carly. "Seriously?"

"I don't mind," she said, smiling and failing to get … well … everything. "Happy to help."

"That's not what I meant."

"What did you mean?"

Thom sighed and looked to Brendan's departing back. "Couldn't you at least have had Brendan wait so I could go with him?"

"I figured you'd want time to cool off. Alone. Usually that's what you want when you're like this."

"'*When I'm like …*'" He dropped it. "Not this time."

"Why?"

Ugh. No way to win. "You're okay with Brendan just being off on his own?"

"He has his phone and I told him to be back at the fountain at one. He knows what'll happen if he misses texts or is late. And he's fourteen. Remember fourteen?"

"Carly …"

"You know that girl he likes? I think her mom teaches a goat yoga class at Yoga Bear, and I think Brendan thinks she tags along. That's the real reason I thought you two should separate."

"Well, what the hell am *I* supposed to do?"

"Jesus, Thom," she said, giving her his *what crawled up your butt?* look. "You're welcome."

FIVE

Rip Daddy

THOM WONDERED whether he was following his son for something to do or because he didn't trust him. The latter, if true, would be stupid. Kids might be maturing faster these days, but while many fourteen-year-olds were already burying the hatchet, Thom doubted his own son knew what to do with his.

Brendan was painfully bad with girls — and like the dog who chases cars, Thom was confident his son wouldn't have a clue of what to do with a female if he ever actually caught one. Someone must've also told him women liked a good sense of humor, because Brendan's flirting was entirely jokes. *Unbearable* jokes. He was the kind of joke-teller who forgot to mention the hook, then went back after the punchline to explain.

A man walks into a building. He says ouch. Oh, wait, the building is a bar. I forgot to tell you that part. So he walked into a bar, like, instead of entering a drinking place, I'm saying it's like he rams his head into a bar by mistake. HAHAHA.

Yeah. That kid wasn't getting laid any time soon.

But with that out of the way, why was he after Brendan if not to intrude on his privacy for the hell of it? It was a dick move. He should let the kid have time with his crush. Maybe they'd hold hands; maybe they'd kiss if Brendan got extraordinarily lucky. It wouldn't go farther than that, especially not in the mall. What was he going to do, bend her over in the yoga window? The goats could climb all over them if they were able to stand the gyration.

"Fuck." Thom sat in a chair outside a free-standing Orange Julius, suddenly ashamed.

A peek through the crowd showed him Brendan getting away, but that was just fine. Rick had gotten his way and Brendan had gotten his way and even Carly, who (let's face it) respected Rick's dignity more than Thom's, had more or less gotten her way.

He was the only one still in a bad mood, but maybe that wasn't the worst thing in the world. Maybe this was like penance. In biblical times he would have had to use a whip to flagellate himself, so he should count himself lucky. He'd honored thy mother and, by force and coercion, was honoring his father as well. He'd get his chance when Rick was dead and Brendan—

Something was happening across a gap in the upper level.

Thom was standing outside Men's Wearhouse, looking over at a group of middle-aged suburbanites milling right outside the LEGO Store. They looked like the mildest of mild-mannered folks, and the group was diverse enough to look staged. Despite the khakis and middle-class haircuts, Thom thought at first that the fight might be racial. Some of the shouts had the timbre of insults, and others a tone of indignation.

As the scene unfolded, Thom heard nuance he'd missed before, and …

No. That wasn't an argument. It was closer to a fight.

And one that was spiraling out of control, by the sound.

Thom stood. He wasn't alone. Others were also standing and staring.

But just before things got good, some change of dynamics boxed in the group's troublemakers and dragged the entire group, discretely, toward the bathroom hallway.

Seconds later, they were gone.

Thom surveyed the mall-goers around him.

Everyone had stopped paying attention. Once the problem was out of sight, the crowd seemed content to forget they'd seen it. They were just people with errands to run and fun to have, and fighting would sour that. They didn't care to investigate anything that was about to soil their day.

But for Thom, who had no errands to run and wasn't having any fun, the incident promised a perfect diversion. He rose and went to quell his curiosity.

As he got closer, his angle to the wide bathroom hallway changed and he was able to see down it.

Peace hadn't returned to the group of diverse suburbanites; they'd just gotten their struggling selves out of the thoroughfare.

Thom, moving faster now, felt his interest increase.

What kept people so incredibly *blah* fighting for

so long? They weren't the kind of folks Fight Club was made for.

So why were they so hands-on now?

It looked like they were holding one of their number back, not keeping two different folks from sparring. It was as if someone wanted to go out and play in the crowd, but the buzzkills around him didn't agree.

He reached the hallway, slipped to one side like a professional eavesdropper, then peeked in when he thought it least likely they'd see him.

The group was holding a small black woman, barely five feet tall and surely unstable in a stiff wind. Two Asian men had her by the arms, a white woman was gripping her waist, and two mixed-race men who looked almost like twins were standing slightly back while seeming uncertain.

"What do we do?" one of the arm-holders asked.

"Call someone!"

"She's … OW, dammit, *Theresa!*"

One of the freestanding men had tried to calm or otherwise touch her, and she'd bitten his finger.

Chomped right down, judging by all the gushing blood.

"Dad?"

Thom looked to his left, so startled that he almost fell over.

Apparently he was nervous. Apparently this scene, so unusual for a mall, had him on-edge.

"Brendan? I thought you were off meeting ..." He remembered the official story and changed course. "I thought you were looking at video games."

"She wasn't there," Brendan said, his mind clearly elsewhere.

He'd noticed the fight down the hallway, and unless Brendan was blind, he'd also noticed the blood, pouring from the man's finger like water from a busted faucet, creating a messy canvas on which the others kept painting with their scrambling feet.

They'd moved quite far down the hallway; that's why only Thom and Brendan, who were lined up just right, could see. It didn't look entirely intentional. Those at the rear were using maybe too much force to hold the raging woman back, causing their overall trajectory to move away.

The madwoman's face was wild, ringlet hair mostly covering her eyes. Her mouth wouldn't close. It stayed open with lips pulled back to display two bared rows of teeth.

"Were you following me?" Brendan asked.

"No," Thom lied, then pointed and told him a truth. "I was just sitting over there."

"What's wrong with her?" Brendan sounded scared.

"I don't know."

"Is it that rabies thing?"

"It's not rabies, Brendan."

"You know what I mean."

Thom considered. He knew Rip Daddy better than most people because he'd made it a morbid obsession. Every second spent reading CDC bulletins, even though the research excursions always left him in stomach-churning agony. He wanted to be prepared. He wanted to know what to do to keep himself and his family safe. And beyond that, once he reached the limit of things he could control, Thom wanted to know just how badly the world was planning to conspire against him.

You were supposed to change the things you could and accept the things you couldn't change, but Thom's life philosophy had him sweating it all. No better way to be paranoid and afraid; that was Thom's motto.

"No, this is something different. Rip Daddy doesn't ... *BRENDAN!*"

A man had emerged from the bathroom, seemingly in there the entire time and unaware of the struggle taking place just beyond the doors. He turned right, toward the mall atrium and away from the corner into which the struggling group had wedged itself.

They were still grunting with their shoes making dolphin sounds on bloody tile, but the noises were too small or the man was too deaf or possibly he just wasn't paying attention. Either way, his distraction was enough to unbalance it all.

One man holding the woman's arm looked up and shouted something, like maybe *CALL SOMEONE!*, but with his attention distracted, the struggler popped her arm free.

A bubble of chaos followed. A second later the woman was fully free, sprinting like crazy.

And Brendan — that little shit — was rushing the new arrival.

At first Thom was paralyzed. People didn't run *toward* danger; people ran *away* from danger.

It was such a fundamental break with sanity that at first Thom couldn't even move. In those moments he literally did not understand. He simply waited with his mouth still open, the last syllable of

"BRENDAN!" held a beat too long before holding position on his lips.

The N sound died, Thom's mouth sagged, and still it'd been no more than two ticks on the overhead clock.

He found his awareness again, too late now to grab his son and pull him back. Not only was Brendan fourteen where Thom was nearly forty, Brendan was also on the track team — the one spring sport Thom would allow him to play.

Hard to hurt yourself running track.

Unless you were running toward insanity.

The bathroom was closer to Thom and Brendan than it was to the group. The man, emerging, was similarly closer to them than to the woman when she spotted fresh prey, broke free, and ran.

The people who'd accidentally let go would never catch the woman before she tackled the newcomer.

Brendan was even closer — and if he moved *now*, he could be the first of everyone. Brendan had seen all of this, deducing that the woman planned to attack, not run past the man or shake his hand, and if he didn't move to prevent it, then the assault was inevitable.

In the second before his scream, Thom realized

he could no longer stop his son from doing something … well, something like his grandfather would do.

You mean, noble? said a voice in Thom's head.

I mean stupid, said another.

The woman couldn't have Rip Daddy. The disease was incapacitating, not aggressive-making.

But clearly she had *something*, and Thom for one wasn't eager to bring it home. You called the authorities when people went nuts in public. You didn't take matters into your own hands.

Moot. All of it. Brendan didn't so much as pause at the man.

He barreled toward the chaos instead.

SIX

Paranoid Fantasies

THOM MOVED FORWARD TOO SLOWLY.

Brendan was already atop the woman, while her original group approached from behind, trying to pin her shoulders the way Coach had taught him that single year he'd wrestled. He'd been good; they'd been thinking scholarship almost immediately. But Thom put the kibosh on it when Brendan sprained a wrist, considering them lucky for aborting when they did.

Carly said, *It's just a wrist.*

And Thom responded, *Exactly. Let's quit while he's ahead.*

But those skills were back in foolish force. Brendan looked a man about to clear a crowd: *Stand back! I'm a trained professional. I'll handle this!*

"Brendan, get off!" Thom cried out.

The others were arriving, but Brendan couldn't enlist help without relaxing his pin.

Soon the area around the woman (with Brendan on top) was all splayed hands on tile: a lot of folks kneeling as if to help, but none of them able to do much of anything.

Thom turned to tell the man Brendan had saved to go and get help, but he was scuttling off like a coward without looking back. Lucky bastard.

Panic flight, Thom thought. *If only that was us.*

"Brendan!"

"Dad, I'm … OW!"

Someone muttered what sounded like an apology. An elbow had struck Brendan on his chin. It seemed okay — he took the blow like a champ and the woman hadn't moved.

But then Brendan winced and the woman found the right leverage.

A second later she was up, with Brendan dazed on the floor behind her.

One of her group finally took charge with gusto; he tackled her outright, no punches pulled, and together the pair skid-rolled into the deserted bathroom, gliding on the drying slick of blood.

The bitten man was still wailing behind

Brendan and Thom. Or so it seemed until his senses returned and Thom realized the bitten man should be *in front of him*, not behind … and that the man wasn't actually wailing.

He looked scared and sheet-white, but no sound was leaving his mouth.

No, that sound was coming from …

Thom and Brendan both looked back at once. Whatever they'd heard was no longer happening. The mall had gone silent, just an average day for American consumers, if they kept their heads turned in that direction.

Or maybe they hadn't heard anything out there. The echoes were strange in here.

"Dad, was that …"

"Go."

"I thought I heard …"

Thom was shoving his son. He had to move Brendan from Hero Pose, then worry about himself.

He looked into the bathroom and saw only thrashing feet, until a fan-spray of blood suddenly bloomed on the exposed wall like impromptu graffiti. Then the feet seemed to shuffle and spin. The attached bodies began to rotate, only now one pair of feet was sluggish and dragging.

Sounds from inside the porcelain chamber had

turned animalistic. The last thing Thom saw before making a decision was the woman, now clearly holding the upper hand, arcing back with a red-smeared face.

A pool of deep crimson was already wide and spreading with menace across the floor.

The man's feet finally stopped moving.

Brendan stood to investigate, but Thom yanked him back.

There were others here. They'd caused this.

"Dad!"

"Get up. Go." Thom kept shoving, not caring what his sloppy, desperate actions must look like.

This was his son in front of him — no more than fifteen feet from either a dead body or one on death's doorstep. There were cops for this; it wasn't a fourteen-year-old's job (or his out-of-shape father's) to handle it. The others were already surrounding the bathroom entrance, all afraid but none leaving a gap. One had already smashed glass to grab a fire axe. Another wrenched a heavy fire extinguisher from the wall.

"GO!"

But of course Brendan was headstrong, like Rick, and he wouldn't go under his own power.

So Thom grabbed him and pulled. Brendan's

feet started to move on the slick floor. Thank God the kid didn't play football. Track stars were lean and light. Thom, meanwhile, had put on more than a few pounds over the past decade. What he lacked in strength, he gained in mass.

Within twenty seconds they were on the edge of the food court, then twenty after that they were back beside the atrium. Outside, everything they'd seen felt like a bad dream. There was no melee here in the real world.

That had been an anomaly in the hallway — enough that a subversive presence inside Thom argued it hadn't really happened at all. That presence suggested he go about his day: *Step aside, folks — nothing to see here.*

The feeling was compulsively strong. Nothing, in the moment, was more tempting to forget. To reaffirm, once and for all, that the world was forever as it should be.

But no. He wasn't quite that cowardly.

"Come on," he said.

"Dad, we have to help!"

"We're helping."

"Someone might get hurt!"

"Someone already got hurt, Brendan. *Two* someones. I don't want anyone else to get hurt either, but even more than that I don't want *you* hurt, son. That was brave of you to go after that woman, but it was stupid, too. The best way we can help is to find someone *better equipped* to—"

"But, Dad—"

"You saw what happened to the guy who tackled her. Someone armed needs to go after her next." He thought of mall cop clichés. "Or at least pepper spray. More than a few semesters of wrestling."

They were moving fast again, Thom with a decent idea where he needed to go. Brendan's combativeness had faded along with his brief spike of adrenaline. Now he was quiet. Almost somber despite all the lights and regular everyday conversations — despite the obscenely early pa-rum-pum-pum-pum of "The Little Drummer Boy" in the background.

They arrived at the mall security office.

Brendan gave his father a look, but the last of his bravado was gone. He still looked strong — still eager to do the right thing — but now he also looked drained. He was probably realizing what Thom already knew. What they'd just seen had been so shocking as to be all-consuming for two minutes of their lives, but still a singular incident.

Any random day of the news would prove there were worse happenings everywhere and all the time.

The world wasn't as high-octane as Thom's pulse kept wanting to insist that it was. This was still just the mall, the frozen-yogurt hassles with his overly obstinate father. They'd seen a problem happen, but being a witness to the event didn't make it their responsibility, and there was no reason for his day to have turned as hostile as it suddenly felt.

A uniformed officer emerged while they were pausing to enter. He looked at them with a mouthful of bagel sandwich, clearly not expecting to find anyone outside. "You guys okay?"

Thom started. "We're okay. But—"

"Someone got attacked!" Brendan yelled.

"What? Where?"

Thom gave Brendan a look. The boy's urge for action was decaying into mania. His glance broadcasted, *Let me handle this*. But to the guard, he said, "There's a group by the bathrooms. One of them—"

"She bit him!"

The guard said, *"What?"*

"A woman," Thom said. "She's … sick with something. It looked a little like—"

"She bit his finger right off!"

"She didn't bite it *off*, Brendan."

Did she?

The guard raised a hand, vying for his turn. "What exactly—"

"Then she ripped this guy's throat out!"

"We don't know what we saw," said Thom, unsure of who he was even speaking to.

"There's blood everywhere, mister," Brendan kept going. "And the guy she bit, the first one with the finger, he was looking crazy right afterward. Like he got the same thing that she got."

"That's not what I saw," said Thom.

"He did! He was looking like he'd do it, too!"

"Do what?" asked the guard.

"Grandpa was saying it in the car, Dad. He said he heard some of those guys, you know from that company? They were talking about something like this. Like some secret formula that's part of the experiment."

"What experiment?" asked the guard.

Thom adopted an apologetic tone not at all appropriate to the emergency situation. "My father is in a drug trial, and he's got Alzheimer's, and he's got these paranoid fantasies that—"

"'Paranoid'? Dad, we saw it happen!"

"—that someone's always doing *experiments* on him, and that the trial he's in is actually a secret *conspiracy*, and—"

The guard's radio exploded with static.

Someone on its other end said something, choked with distortion, that Thom couldn't hear. But the guard did; he pressed a button on the mouthpiece clipped to his left-side epaulette and said he'd be right there.

"Someone else saw it?" Thom asked.

"No, no, nothing to worry about. Someone fell down near the Macy's, is all."

Another burst on the radio. Thom heard the word *paramedics*. A few seconds later he swore he heard the word *Hemisphere*, too.

"I have to go," said the guard.

"It's not by the Macy's. It's by the food court bathrooms."

"Yeah. I'll look into it." He was already filing it under *B-level Tasks*, far behind his more-urgent slip-and-fall.

"*What if it's zombies,* Dad? I heard one of those people in Rosedale was stabbed but didn't die, or something, and Grandpa was telling me tons and tons of stuff about how *he* saw—"

"Brendan!"

But the damage was done. The guard was already telling them to go inside and file a report if they wanted; someone would be with them shortly.

Thom shouted for the guard to come with them. What they'd seen was a big deal — and real, and involving none of Rick's supernatural, horror-movie dementia bullshit.

In reply, Thom clearly heard the guard say, "Yeah, yeah."

When the guard was gone, Thom opened his mouth to tell Brendan to keep the crazy-ass theories to himself and stick to the facts. They'd gone for help, and spouting off was no way to get it.

But the nightmare started before he could speak.

SEVEN

Diagnosed With a Mental Illness

RICK HEARD a bellowing wail coming from down the Macy's corridor.

It started, then stopped, and for almost a full minute after, it was as if there'd been nothing at all. Everything, in that minute, just sort of returned to normal.

Rosie was watching him. "What is it, Rick?"

His eyes went to Carly, watching but not really. She was checking her phone at the fountain. Or more likely, judging by the sideways way she held it, playing that game she always liked to dick around with. She probably hadn't even heard the scream. Carly had a way of hyper-focusing. Of blocking things out.

"That scream," he said. "Did you hear it?"

Rosie looked, but there was nothing to see. "No."

"It sounded like someone's hurt."

"I didn't hear anything." With the issue closed, Rosie's face cleared of any lingering trouble and she lowered her head back over the yogurt. She'd gotten lemon, nothing mixed in. "This is lovely. Not overpowering at all."

"I think I should check it out."

"Check what out?"

"That scream."

"I didn't hear a scream."

"Rosie, I'm telling you, I heard something. Someone in trouble."

Rosie's reply was a period at the end of the conversation's sentence: "Well, this is the first I'm hearing about it."

Rick stood. He looked toward Carly, but her eyes were still down on the screen.

"After this, we should go to Penney's."

"Penney's is gone, Rose. It went out of business."

"What? When did that happen?"

"April, I think."

"Well, then. Macy's. I want to get some brown shoes."

"What?"

"Brown shoes. I'm so embarrassed."

"Why?"

"Well, look at the shoes I had to wear today. Because they were all I had."

Rick didn't want to look at Rosie's shoes. All his old battle triggers were being activated and he couldn't say why. His first theory was instinct. Despite the mall's normal appearance, sounds, and feel, he'd sensed something amiss for a solid ten minutes, and the scream he'd heard (or at least *thought* he'd heard) was icing on the preparedness cake. The second theory was far less exciting, and Rick blamed Thom for it even being in his head: that the mall *was* normal, *nothing* was amiss, and the errant scream he'd seemed to hear hadn't actually come. Sounds were squirrelly that way. Once they were gone, they were gone. There was no way short of a recording to prove they'd even happened.

He looked at Rosie's shoes anyway. Every nerve in his body was telling him that he needed to prepare for a rumble, but he still had that sneaking suspicion — a trifle of a possibility, really, and no more — that it was all an illusion.

Thom's suspicions about Rick's forgetfulness had been followed by Thom's putting Rick in a home, and at the time Rick could even see why. He *had* been forgetful and dazed back then, and maybe he really *had* suffered from Alzheimer's. But that was no longer true.

The Hemisphere doctors had scanned him and proven as much. There were plaques in his brain, they'd explained at the outset. The BioFuse injections they gave him couldn't ever change that. Instead, it would teach his brain how to grow *new* pathways, letting him think *around* the disease-causing plaques.

They ordered him to keep his mouth shut about it. They told him it was a big secret and that they'd deny anything he tried leaking to the public. Of course Rick had blabbed anyway, but his talk had backfired. Instead of being impressed at his father's cure, Thom had told Rick it was just another one of his paranoid fantasies.

What's more likely, Dad? Thom had asked during their inevitable argument. *That a multi-billion-dollar corporation has shifted its work around you because you're so special, complete with secret agents who circle you in black sunglasses and blacker helicopters, threatening you into secrecy? Or is it, instead, more likely that as a man diag-*

nosed with a mental illness, this is all taking place in your head?

Rick didn't buy Thom's way of seeing things for two reasons: because his own eyes and ears and brain told him that his son was wrong and he was right, but also because the idea of being so fundamentally deceived by your own senses was so totally terrifying. He preferred to believe and go down swinging if he had to eventually fall.

But he wasn't an illogical man. Rick understood that Alzheimer's did exactly what Thom described, even if he was convinced the disease wasn't presently doing it to him. So there was a shadow of possibility, and that shadow was what made Rick hesitate even when he was otherwise sure.

Sure he was being followed by apparitions in long coats, sure that strange doings were afoot, sure it was really Miles Pope's voice (and, increasingly, the voices of others) he kept hearing in his head.

And it was, in the food court after that scream and thick sense of danger, the thing that made Rick look at Rosie's shoes as if nothing was the matter. Every nerve was alive, but what if he was wrong?

As much as he hated it — as much as he hated the notion that maybe sometimes Thom was right while Rick was incorrect — he at least owed rationality the benefit of the doubt.

"What about your shoes?"

"They're white!"

"So?"

"It's after Labor Day!"

Rick looked up again at the Macy's corridor. There was still nothing obviously wrong, but a subliminal beat kept insisting that the foot-traffic patterns had changed. More were now coming out than going in, and there was an unusual rush to the egress.

Like watching a platoon run from a napalmed jungle — early stages, not yet at panic.

"Okay." Rick had been standing over his chair, not fully committed.

He stepped away from it, glancing at still-oblivious Carly and putting a hand on Rosie's back. Other than a few quick glances at his immediate surroundings (Rosie, Carly, his feet to make sure he didn't trip while stepping over the chair's seat), he didn't move his eyes away from the corridor.

"Okay, Rosie. You want some brown shoes, let's get you some brown shoes."

"At Penney's?"

"Penney's is closed."

"What? When?"

He guided her up, sparing another glance. "Come on. We can go somewhere else."

"Dillards?"

"Actually," Rick said, guiding her away from the table and toward the escalator, eyeing Carly and moving fast, "I was thinking we'd try Macy's."

EIGHT

Government Plates

SHOUTS AND SCREAMS erupted from everywhere.

Then everything seemed to happen at once. One second he was holding the door and preparing to enter the security office. The next, the officers were coming to him same as the first one had, when he'd surprised him eating lunch.

They didn't ask what Thom needed. They ordered him out of the way.

Thom shouted while they gathered outside, first indignantly (he was a customer, after all), then with frustration and a plunging sense of what-the-hell when they stopped gathering and started running.

He had no idea what to do. None of the guards were armed, and yet they were rushing and running in ways that didn't exactly shout "pepper spray and detainment." Some of them even stayed on the upper level and sprinted through the crowd toward Macy's, while others rushed down the stairs and escalators toward The Cheesecake Factory and dome-topped playground at one of the mall's several middles.

Nobody, Thom saw, was going where he'd instructed.

Nobody was headed toward the food court or its bloody hallway.

Thom heard a few screams coming from that direction, but it was slowly falling apart.

"What's going on, Dad?" Brendan asked.

"I don't know."

"Is it … like … terrorists or something?"

That was a step up from zombies, but equally ridiculous. Not that much made sense right now. Thom realized as they waited that he'd already rapid-repressed something back at the bathrooms — something he didn't want to remember and definitely didn't want to drop in Brendan's mental hopper as chum for nightmares.

The person who'd grabbed the fire axe back there … Thom was pretty sure he'd seen a big downward swing as they'd been turning to run. He was also pretty sure that, once they'd started running, he'd see that same biter up and stumbling with that very same axe in her back.

But no. That hadn't really happened.

"I don't know, Brendan."

"What ..." Now just a kid again, scared and turning to his father. Not that Thom had much to offer. "What should we do? Hide?"

"We have to find your mother. And Grandpa and Rosie."

Their heads whipped in the other direction, and down to the lower level.

"Let's go."

Rushing down the stairs, Thom tried to find a balance between rational actions and terror-flight. He didn't want to overblow the situation (there were a lot of guards, and though they didn't have guns, they had numbers and could, of course, always call the police), but he also didn't want to treat the situation too lightly.

The authorities should be able to handle whatever-it-was. The area had been entirely peaceful and ordinary only moments ago, so what possibly could have gone so wrong? The only thing that'd threaten everyone would be something like a gunman (but then why were they running in several directions) or … and this made sense in a weird way … a fire.

"Dad?" Brendan had caught him thinking.

"I'll bet it's just a fire."

"Just?"

"An electrical fault. Someone dropped a cigarette. Some asshole, playing tricks."

"But that woman we saw—"

Thom was rolling; it was the only way to keep his feet churning. Truth, in Thom's opinion, was overrated. Belief could be practical. Yes, Brendan's point was valid. The woman they saw was definitely not a fire. But at the same time, if Thom let himself wonder if all those scrambling guards were for incidents like her, he might totally lose his mind. Of course it wasn't a fire; he couldn't smell smoke and everyone was running everywhere, not clearly from one place or toward the exits.

But still Thom forced himself to believe it.

It's a fire. Just an ordinary fire.

"Quiet, Brendan. It's a fire."

Brendan didn't look like he agreed even a little. But he was obedient, and stayed beside his father all the way down, all the way across the atrium toward the fountain. Thom spied the yogurt stand, in front of which half a dozen tall stools had been upended and were lying like pick-up sticks. No employees or customers. A few folks were in as much denial as Thom, some milling about the area and a few sipping coffees where they'd always been.

But there were no customers by the yogurt place. No Rick, no Rosie.

And, turning his head, Thom saw that there was no Carly by the fountain, either.

"Dad?"

"She's with them. Of course she's with them. She'd have to be with them. That's what she said."

"Dad?"

Brendan sounded worried — more than before.

"They went outside. Right? They went outside." Thom turned his head. A long line of brown-painted exit doors lined the wall. They were back exits, not the showy front ones. He looked in time to see one easing closed.

Yes, people had gone that way. It was right nearby; the builders had put those exits off the main space to allow easy evacuation in the case of incidents (fires) such as this.

"They'd go outside if there was a fire."

"But Dad … How can it be a fire if—?"

Thom dragged Brendan toward the doors.

He was sure they'd have locked behind the last

one to leave because that's the way things always happened in the movies. When a way out was needed, all exits were blocked. But naturally the doors had been placed for exactly this purpose and were, when pushed from the inside, almost for-sure kept unlocked.

Fresh air — cool in the shade, promising autumn in earnest — kissed his skin.

There was a crowd out here, but smaller than he'd imagined. It wasn't hard to scan them all and see he was wrong. Carly and the others weren't anywhere in sight.

"She went to the car."

"She didn't go to the car, Dad."

"Of course she did. She wouldn't stay in the mall. We have to get to the car." Thom's eyes wandered and, in the spacey few seconds that followed, he realized from outside himself that he was probably in shock.

It was odd to behave one way, then see that same behavior from above.

He was being crazy. He thought there was a fire, and so he ran scared.

The thought alone jostled him. Could he really be the wuss his father always said he was?

Right now, his reasoning was sound. Carly,

Rick, and Rosie were absolutely together, and if they were together then of course they would head for the exit. Why would they do anything else?

His theory was hitting a logjam already. The car, near as Thom could tell with his shoddy sense of direction, was clear on the mall's other side and up a level thanks to uneven sloping of the surrounding ground. It wasn't a short walk, and as much as Rick blustered, walking was agony on his bad leg. But he could do it, and for that reason Thom might have kept right on thinking they'd simply hoofed it around the building. Rosie wasn't fast; she moved and looked like Thom remembered both of his grandmothers at the end. With her in tow, they *couldn't* all run. Carly would have to trust them together for as long as it took for her to the car …

Nope. There were two problems with that, Thom was already starting to see.

He had the keys, not Carly. She could go to the car, but she wouldn't have any way of driving it back.

It also didn't make sense to exit here and rendezvous all the way over there. Carly would want to wait for her husband and son, and this was the most logical place to do so. Even if they'd decided to walk around, the speed limit imposed by Rosie and Rick should make them visible.

The mall couldn't have been evacuated that quickly.

"DAD!"

Thom looked. Brendan was extending his phone, waiting for his father to either look or take it.

He wasn't sure what he was seeing at first, but then he noted the open app on Brendan's phone and understood. Carly wanted him to live as a free-range teen, arguing that kids needed their autonomy and therefore tracking their son like a lost dog would be an invasion of independence and privacy.

Of course Thom had won that battle and Brendan had been on an invisible tether ever since getting his phone, but the street ran both ways. The same app let Brendan see where his parents were, too. As Thom zoomed in, he saw the dot indicating Carly's dot not circling the mall, but still inside it.

"The GPS isn't perfect," he told the screen. "There's a margin of error."

But the GPS's margin, though theoretically in place, had never applied as far as Thom had seen. Sometimes when Carly parked to run in and grab something from the grocery store, he sat in the car and watched her, able to tell when she reached the meat counter, when she ran past the dairy, when she tore through the frozen aisle.

Right now her dot said she was in the Macy's corridor. That was where he thought he'd heard that second set of screams — where half of the rushing security guards had gone. And now he couldn't get the chills to vacate his body.

Thom shook off his fear. Native or not, there was no time. Nobody else was going to be in charge here. It was him or nothing. "I have to go back in for her."

"What about Grandpa and Rosie?"

"I'm sure they're all together."

He *hoped* they were all together. Rick didn't have a phone; one of his paranoid regulars was a certainty that all phones spied on their users. Unlike most of his conspiracy theories, that wasn't an especially delusional notion. Thom knew that was at least mostly true.

They might have been separated.

(They also might be dead.)

But that was crazy talk. So Thom pushed it away, not truly disbelieving it so much as unwilling to consider something so ridiculous. There was really no reason for anyone to be dead (except the man who got attacked by the biter, plus maybe the biter thanks to that axe in her back), and a single crazy person wasn't, statistically speaking, dangerous enough to fear.

Except that there was more than one.

And now he could never ignore it, thanks to what he'd already seen of the distributed chaos inside.

Thom jogged for the exit doors with Brendan on his heels. He turned around and said, "You stay here."

"I don't want to stay here."

"Do as I say!"

Brendan heard him. He was usually an obedient kid who listened to what his parents told him to do. But still he acted deaf.

Thom put a hand on the door handle. "You want to help? Call 911. When someone shows up, tell them what you saw, then stick close to them. I'll look for the sirens when I come out."

"No."

"No?"

Thom moved between Brendan and the door, then channeled paternal anger like never before. A primal emotion, deep down where does sacrifice themselves for their fawns, and bucks spar to ensure the endurance of their genes over another's.

"Get out of here, Brendan. *Now.*"

His son seemed near compliance, but the door Thom had tugged on wasn't opening. He looked and saw no latch — just a lock. Of course. These were utility doors, not a main entrance.

"Maybe if you wait for someone else to come out," Brendan suggested.

So Thom waited. Three seconds. Four. It was taking an eternity, and he couldn't move his eyes away from the pulsing blue dot indicating Carly's position. It kept moving; that felt like a good sign. But it could also be GPS inaccuracy again, and in truth her phone might be stationary after all, possibly two floors down with its screen smashed while his wife's body, prone far above and bloodied by attack, dangled with one hand—

"Nobody's coming out."

"It's been like five seconds."

Thom looked right, ran long the building, then scrambled up a slope high on nature and low on landscaping. He came through a bush, then saw that he could easily have circled around it and emerged without scratches. Brendan came up behind him.

"I told you to stay. Why aren't you listening to me?"

When Brendan didn't answer, there was nothing to rebuff.

He rushed on around the big building and his son kept pace behind him.

Thom stopped suddenly. He reached out and grabbed Brendan's arm before the boy could rush past him and assume the lead. He pulled them against the building, behind a line of succulents and decorative tufts of grass.

"What?" Brendan asked.

"Do you recognize those vans?"

He looked. Then shook his head. "Just vans, Dad."

And they *were* just vans, but they bothered Thom nonetheless. For one, there were five, all identical and parked in a cluster. Second, Thom and Brendan hadn't made it around to an entrance yet, and their position now was at another set of emergency rear doors — this time for the new holiday store occupying the defunct Penney's.

Something bothered him about those five identical vans, parked against an exit instead of an entrance. And no matter what Brendan recognized or didn't, Thom found them oddly familiar, would bet just about anything that he'd seen them before.

Behind me on the drive over? Didn't Rick say one of his "followers" was a van?

Maybe. Thom crept closer, keeping an eye out for … for anything, he supposed.

Government plates, plain as a tax form.

So they were government vehicles?

But no; now that Thom was close enough, he saw HEMISPHERE in slightly-off paint along the sides — the kind of job that marked "unmarked" police cars, so you could only see the writing on their sides once it was already too late for escape.

The company's motto was printed below it, just as hard to see: UPGRADING NATURE.

Subtle paint.

Hemisphere vans.

Five of them. Parked out back. With government plates.

Brendan ran a hand over the cool metal side of the closest van. They seemed to be empty. "*Hemisphere*," he read, then looked at his father. "Isn't that the name of those people doing that test thing with Grandpa?"

Thom didn't so much as nod, but yes, that's exactly what Hemisphere was. He'd researched the hell out of the company before agreeing to Rick's BioFuse trial. A poor man's background check before the group entered his extended family's life.

From what Thom had seen, they were both forward-thinking and aggressive in their approach — something Thom had appreciated at the time. Hemisphere was close to curing a dozen or more diseases the wider world had already given up on, and at the same time they were overflowing with proactive research — human optimization, telomere treatments that were supposed to slow aging, and more.

The last one, Thom was perfectly willing to believe. Hemisphere's poster boy and CEO, Archibald Burgess, was supposedly in his upper seventies but looked fifty, and a muscular and vibrant half-century at that. The press found him obnoxious, but Thom saw him as refreshing. He'd seen a lot of obnoxious doctors with Carly's group. Men and women who couldn't admit to being fallible, so sure they were right that the literature was overflowing with patients who died of a doctor's arrogance more than any disease.

Doctors were afraid of being sued, walking a line between "too conservative" and "not conservative enough." But Burgess wasn't a doctor. He was a businessman, with an engineer's brain. A man after Thom's own heart.

"Come on," Thom said.

When they made it to the marquee entrance, they found more familiar vans. Bakersfield PD, and even a SWAT unit with its rear doors open, its members approaching the building.

Thom waved Brendan in a far circle, looking at the GPS app the entire time, until they were past the cops and to a smaller, secondary entrance nearly another third of the way around the building. The only upside was that this entrance was right past the food court. It was the closest to Carly's dot that they were going to get.

At the door, Thom turned again to Brendan. "Stay out here."

"Alone?"

"Hide over there." He pointed. "Brendan? Listen to me. This is really important. Don't think you're not helping by being here. If they come out, you need to make sure you tell them to stay put. If you're not here, they could run out and we'll just end up in a circle."

"But we can see that Mom's phone ..." He pointed to the app.

"Grandpa doesn't have a phone and neither

does Rosie. We can't be sure they're together. Your grandfather gets confused sometimes, and Rosie's kind of in the clouds all the time. If she's alone and she comes out here and nobody's around to get her . . ."

"Okay," Brendan said. "I understand."

"I'll be fast."

He moved out. Brendan called to him.

Thom turned back around. "What?"

"My phone. You've got my phone."

Feeling seconds tick away, he looked at the phone. Thom never configured his own tracker app. He'd always used Carly's, and truth be told he'd never been great at tech — embarrassing for an engineer. But then again he was a *civil* engineer and not an *electronic* engineer or computer scientist, so he was, more often than not, free to be every bit the philistine he naturally was.

He pulled out his own phone and threw it to Brendan, pausing mid-arc to realize the boy would probably drop and break the thing. But he caught it just fine.

Thom said, "Set up the app and watch us, okay?"

He looked around for a weapon, still wanting to believe this was a fire. But the more disturbing possibilities were starting to look a lot more possible. Police might come for a fire, but SWAT never would. He should really be armed if he was foolish enough to reenter the mall. But how?

A pile of fencing supplies sat not far off — remnants of recent construction. Thom grabbed a short length of aluminum pipe, tested its heft and swing, then re-pocketed Brendan's phone to free both hands.

Then he nodded at his son and entered the mall.

NINE

What If?

IT WAS TOO STILL INSIDE.

The mall, when empty, had a low echo that existed almost below the level of human detection. Its emptiness and recent desertion had left their own ghosts, giving the place the creepy feel of a liminal space.

He could hear drips coming from the food court. Perhaps someone's beverage had overturned on the table and was now leaking to the floor. Now and then he heard shuffling. Human feet, probably, but in this cavernous space the proportional sound was more like roaches under the baseboards, or mice hiding in the walls.

He tilted his head, listening for more screams. He'd heard them coming from all over, Thom had decided while outside. He just hadn't tuned in; he hadn't had the context to believe it. But now back inside, he knew those yells were missing. Three sets from different places.

The fact that none remained seemed to mean one of two things. Either there was nothing left to fear here (something the abundant police presence outside appeared to contradict) or those who'd been screaming were no longer able to make any noise.

After all, it hadn't been the teeth-gnashing woman earlier who'd sounded like a roomful of crashing instruments. The cacophony had belonged to her companions. The man who'd gushed blood from his neck had been belting out a series of deafening bellows, right up until the second before his feet finally stopped moving.

Could be the same reason for all the silence now?

Thom saw activity and ducked, realizing it was a team of cops in riot masks. They had their guns drawn and were moving like a SEAL team. Four of them, heading toward the same hallway where Thom and Brendan had lived through a nightmare.

Thom, destined for the Macy's, stayed low to let them pass.

He crept forward again once he thought they

were gone. Thom believed he was alone, but here and there he began to see eyes in corners, underneath tables and benches and in-store displays.

They were people — shoppers — hiding to wait out whatever-this-was. A few widened eyes looked at him like a savoir, but whenever Thom caught their attention he made the universal gesture to lay low and be cool — a slow, horizontal patting-down of the air.

Near a suite of lobby massage chairs, Thom ducked again.

This time the people sneaking through the space weren't cops, or in SWAT gear. A man and a woman, both in black suit coats with skinny black ties. They were armed, holding strange, bell-ended weapons that reminded Thom of a Civil War-era blunderbuss. The things were somewhere between shotgun and pistol-length. Closer to MAC-10 size but all chrome and boxy casing.

Something moved inside the nearby sporting goods store.

The woman turned and aimed her weapon at the disturbance. The air filled with a sound like a come-here whistle, and at its end a garment rack leapt up from the ground, then crumpled upon landing as if squeezed by a giant hand.

She pulled up immediately, seeing a trio of teenage girls who'd been hiding near the rack rush to take cover somewhere more substantial. The woman lowered her weapon, and the besuited gentleman leaned in to say something to her. The pair moved on, leaving Thom with a heavily furrowed brow.

Once inside Macy's, Thom found himself at the limit of his clues. The GPS dot was now covering his entire immediate area. He was well within its margin of error — now more like *in the margin of error of the margin of error*. It wasn't a map to his wife's phone. It had simply pointed him in the right direction.

"Carly!" Thom hissed to the empty store.

His tried texting. No response.

The phone issued a strange sound.

Swearing and scrambling, he moved to mute the thing, sure he'd just been given away to …

Well, to what? Only now did Thom stop to think that he had no idea what he was fleeing, or any clue as to what he thought might grab him. He'd seen that woman go nuts, of course, but that was an isolated whacko. What had cleared the entire mall, seemingly from three directions at once?

Bizarre as it seemed, this entire experience had the feel of a siege. If the mall was a military target, the situation almost made sense. The enemy creates an ambush from all sides.

But the mall was still just a mall and not a target at all.

And what of the crazy woman? How did she factor into this?

Thom looked at his phone. It seemed Brendan had gotten the app working outside and was now sending him a message directly through it rather than through text. No wonder he hadn't recognized the notification sound.

Thom read the message. *Come out if you find Mom and Grandpa. I saw Rosie.*

What did it mean to *see* Rosie? Did he mean he'd *found* Rosie? That he *had* Rosie?

Thom didn't want to try and figure out the new messaging system, so he switched to text and replied, *I haven't found them yet.*

His phone rang again — a different chirp this time, because apparently he hadn't muted it after all. The context of the ring was strange, but Thom understood why when he looked at the screen.

He'd texted Brendan, but *he* had Brendan's phone. The sound that came back was his own text returning home. The notification was the same as the custom ring Brendan had set for his parents. An obnoxious animal sound that Thom absolutely hated. A narwhal breaching for air, or something.

"Brendan?" came a voice.

"Carly?"

"Thom?"

Carly stood from behind a checkout counter.

Then she came to him, grasped him briefly, and said, "I've been texting you."

"Brendan has my phone."

She looked at the phone in Thom's hand, in its bright blue case. "So I see. Is he safe?"

"He's outside." Thom looked at the screen to confirm, and saw that *Dad* (really Brendan, with Thom's phone) had shown up outside the mall instead of back at home where his dot had been since everyone else had configured their apps.

"What happened here?" Thom asked.

"I think there's a wild animal loose."

"What?"

"I know. But I heard all this growling and … Oh, shit." Carly's voice threatened to break before she reeled it in. "Thom, I went past this guy and he was … God."

Thom told her about his and Brendan's adventures in the hall near the bathroom.

"You think this was a *person?* A *person* did this?"

"I only know what I saw." Something was wrong. He squinted. "Where's Rick?"

"They ran off."

"Ran off!"

"Don't give me shit right now, Thom; I can't take it!"

He waved her down. "Fine. Okay. Where did you see him last?"

"Don't yell. Down by the yogurt place. They both slipped away."

"They—!" But he'd tacitly promised not to yell, so he breathed slowly instead. "Okay. Both of them?"

"They both got away. I assume they're together."

Thom raised Brendan's phone and sent a text outside: *Is Grandpa with Rosie?*

No.

She's alone?

Yes.

Are you sure?

When are you coming out?

Carly was waiting.

Thom didn't answer, then forgot outright to respond, looking at Carly instead. "I think there's an exit back there."

"We're on the top level."

He nodded. "It's okay. I came in at the top level. The ground is higher on this side. Do you think we should look around for Rick first, or …"

"He'd be with Rosie," Carly told him.

"Brendan said he wasn't."

"He must have been at first, at least. I doubt he's here."

Thom nodded decisively. Rick, even when slightly senile, was more than capable of taking care of himself. Their son was the bigger issue, as was the frail old woman in their care. They were both outside.

"Okay. We'll go out. If we can't find Rick, we'll … Well, we'll cross that bridge when we come to it." He raised the fence post, then looked around. The area was still and quiet.

"That way." He pointed.

Carly hesitated.

"What?"

"That's where I saw the body."

Thom looked. "That way?"

She nodded.

"It's the way out," he told her.

"I know."

"It's just a body. Don't look. Do you remember where it is?"

She nodded.

"*Exactly* where?"

Another nod.

Thom made his voice far more sure and strong than he felt. "Okay. So here's what we do. You know where it is, so just don't look there. Move your eyes anywhere else. Focus on the exit door. In fact … See it? Behind where it says *Children's*?"

"Yes."

"Keep your eyes there, and not where you saw … the thing. I'll watch your steps for you. Don't worry, okay? I got this."

The words *I got this*, coming from Thom, sounded all wrong. It was too bold a thing to say — too take-charge for the Thoms of the world. Still, somehow, it fit neatly in this moment. Carly must have wanted to believe that her husband was strong. Thom, for his part, kept trying to forget that he wasn't. The message came off as necessary rather than cheesy.

Carly took his unencumbered arm. Thom

would need it back if he had to start swinging, but for now the store was still and the way seemed more or less clear. There might be someone hiding in between with ill intent, but he didn't think so. The woman Thom had seen earlier hadn't been subtle or quiet. If she or someone like her was in the room, he felt fairly confident he'd know in plenty of time.

They passed one rack after another. Despite his self-assurances, Thom startled at every shadow, sure something was going to spring out like a bag snatcher on Halloween. The sensation didn't even make sense. The mall was deserted; it just felt all wrong because malls were only supposed to be empty when they were closed with all the gates rolled down.

Having a department store open, with all the lights on, and the abandoned belongings of departed shoppers dropped haphazardly on the floor … it was odd enough to jar the loose screws inside his head.

Worse, it was dawning on Thom that he didn't actually know what he was supposed to be afraid of. This dizzy feeling had started with the insane woman going nuts and turning cannibal on her friend, but wasn't she peripheral to what was happening now, with everyone running, with the SWAT and police?

They wouldn't have called all those people for one woman, no matter how out of control she might have been. So what else was happening here? He'd heard screams from this direction and thought they were part of the same scrap, suggesting that whatever happened here at least sounded like what Thom had seen.

But … What?

Was there another like the crazy woman? Were there two of them?

Or, judging by the action he'd seen, *maybe even three?*

Ridiculous. Crazy people didn't coordinate. Robbers and terrorists did, same for crazies planning to stage a mass shooting. But try as he might, it was near impossible for Thom to imagine that woman gathering two of her friends and all of them agreeing on a single plan for unmitigated insanity.

I'll bite off fingers by the food court. Chuck, you bite off fingers at the Macy's. Meet at the getaway car. Got it? Good.

Thom didn't have to know. What he had to do was get the hell out of here. It'd been easy enough the first time. But now he had Carly, and the exit was thirty feet away, with Brendan and Rosie outside. His father could be anywhere, but that was Rick. He would either be fine on his own or somehow manage to die gloriously.

Icing on the cake if they managed to find him.

"Almost done," Thom whispered under his breath.

Then it became a mantra. He said it to calm his nerves, trying hard to believe it was true.

"What?" Carly asked.

"I was saying we're almost there."

Her fingernails bit into his flesh as she gasped. "The body."

Oh, Thom thought, *that.* He saw the direction of her gaze from the corner of his eye and made an executive decision not to join her. She wasn't supposed to be looking down; Thom was supposed to be doing that for her. But he hadn't been looking. Thom been daydreaming — or whatever this was.

Now Carly had seen the thing she didn't want to see and that was too bad, but at least it meant he could stop looking out for it. Judging by her trembling hands, he'd already decided it would be grotesque beyond words. No need to look, if she already had.

"It's okay," he said, feigning calm. "It's only a body."

"Thom."

He looked, not wanting to.

Then he understood why her voice had gone so strange.

She wasn't unnerved by the body she'd seen; Carly's unseating came from a horrifying bloodstain on a rack of fall dresses that would have looked hideous even without the patterns of plasma.

He looked, not wanting the punchline.

"Where did it go?" Carly asked.

"I'm sure you're just remembering wrong."

"I'm not remembering wrong." But she sounded upset, almost hysterical. She looked around to be sure, then began to point as she talked. "I was over there. I thought I saw them come this way, and when I was standing there, I looked that way and saw that big poster. That one. It reminded me of Rosie, too."

Thom followed her finger, his eyes settling near the activewear where a large brand advert showed a whole cluster of active seniors, a few with white hair just like Rosie's.

"But then I looked over here because I thought someone was fighting. I … yes, *look!* I saw this SALE sign and thought maybe a couple of girls were fighting over the last bargain something. That was there. They knocked over a bunch of racks, see?"

Thom saw. He saw the bloodstain again, too. It was so large, he couldn't picture anyone who'd created it ever shopping again.

"It was here, Thom. I'm sure of it. This crazy man just … he just sort of leapt on this woman all at once! A bunch of people tried to stop him, but he wouldn't let go. And then …" Her voice faltered; this was the part she'd been keeping down, trying not to relive until she was safely away. "He … Thom, he just started *biting* her! Like a dog! He clamped down, and no matter how many times this one man hit him with … See that stripped rack over there? He hit the guy over and over, and after enough hits the biting guy … his scalp just kind of peeled away. He …" She stopped herself before Thom could.

Carly looked like she might be sick.

"It's okay," he said uselessly.

"But then the guy, the biting guy, he just pulled back and there was this … this *chunk of HER* between his teeth. It came away all …" Again she stopped. Thom understood this part and nodded. He'd seen almost exactly the same thing, but in a different part of the mall, and with a different culprit.

"I know."

"You don't know!"

"I know, Carly. We saw it, too."

"You were here?"

"No, we were … It doesn't matter. Forget the body. We need to get the hell out of this place."

Thom felt it, too — like a hand at his back. As a kid, knowing better, he used to fear monsters under the bed. He was too old for such fears, and Rick would have mocked him endlessly if he'd caught Thom in the grips of his delusion.

Although, "compulsion" was maybe a better word. Little Thomas knew just fine that no dead and ghostly hand was going to reach from under the bed to grab his ankle right before his second leg rose to the mattress, but still he couldn't help but wonder, *What if?*

It was always best to move quickly just in case.

His feet moved, but Carly's were dragging.

Their hands parted, and Thom moved to more firmly grip his improvised bat.

"It was right here," she said.

"The biter? Or the bitten?"

"The bitten. Although …" Carly started to

wander. Just a few racks away, but still.

"Carly. Come on."

"The biter ran after the guy who'd been hitting him after he lost interest in this one." She pointed at the bloodstain. "I thought I heard him fall down the escalator."

Carly was at the escalator. Thom couldn't see the bottom from where he was, but her body language said there was nothing down there, either.

"What happened to them?" she asked.

"Does it really matter?"

It was like she couldn't hear him. "Why are the bodies gone? I'm sure this one was definitely dead and the other almost had to be. Even if she was somehow still alive, I don't see how far she could possibly ..."

Carly looked around the store with an investigator's gaze. Then she returned to the bloodstain and knelt down next to it, looking close but not touching.

Thom tried not to see the large chunk of what must be flesh near a wrinkle in one of the befouled dresses. He tried not to smell the air, which reeked of copper.

"What's going on here?" Carly asked him.

But he never got a chance to answer.

TEN

Radioactive With Abnormality

Thom wanted to scream but couldn't.

Something was suddenly crawling through the rack next to Carly, unseen and apparently in no hurry.

For a terrifying moment, his mouth refused to work. He couldn't form words; he couldn't scream for Carly to watch out; he couldn't even make his muscles obey, to reach down and pull her back.

For *one one thousand, two one thousand*, Thom could only gape while his heart slammed tribal rhythms into his chest.

He couldn't stop looking at the thing. Human, but not human at all. The body belonged to a teenage boy not much older than Brendan, and from what Thom could see, all the right parts were where they should be. The kid looked like he'd slammed his forearm against something sharp because it had bled through his torn sleeve and dried, but otherwise he could have been an upperclassman at his son's school, no different from any other.

But through that abject normality, something was practically radioactive with abnormality.

The eyes were ordinary — green, Thom thought — but there was no light in them. The mouth was like any other, but it hung open like meat hanging off of a bone. The breathing was all wrong, too; it sounded like something about to expire all alone. The reek on its breath was decay wafting from below the killing floor of a slaughterhouse. This boy, Thom knew, was not a boy at all.

Then a thought occurred to him, and it came in the blink of an eye before action consumed him.

A boy? Carly's story didn't mention a boy.

But then sense and strength returned, and he pulled Carly away from the creeping thing that was no longer a boy if it had ever even been one at all. She only saw it once fully upright, and by then it was a demon in the sewer — looking up at her, curious, temporarily bound by the rack it'd been crawling through.

It studied them with a growl. A hideous rattle that portended bones broken loose inside. A phlegmy sound. The rolling, roiling feel of a semi-solid, like Jell-O in the throat.

Carly screamed. She startled, toppling racks, just managing to stay on her feet. Screams came from elsewhere as well, human and horrible. Thom had to assume there were others hiding, seeing this, not having thought to run or finding themselves unable.

"THE DOOR!"

Because there was another one coming.

The screams had rung some sort of dinner bell. The new creature's scalp was so bashed in, it looked like a bowl of freshly made salsa. Thom thought it might be the biter Carly had mentioned, but right now nothing mattered less in the world.

That door up ahead was the only thing in the universe worth anything to him right now. Carly had taken his point and was preceding toward it, careless of what she had to leap or crash through to get from A to Z.

Someone — a normal man, by the look, rushed

the salsa guy from behind. He had a handgun, apparently flouting the mall's clearly posted concealed-carry restriction. Thom watched the man shout to nab the creature's attention, then fired three slugs through its chest.

He pulled the trigger a fourth time but elicited only dry clicks.

The slide had locked open but still the would-be savior kept pulling the trigger, now frozen in place.

You should be dead, Thom thought of the thing, bleeding pre-clotted blood onto the patterned carpet. *He shot you through the lungs and heart.*

But the creature didn't even slow. It wasn't fast, but the gunman was so thoroughly baffled, he hadn't even tried to run. The next bit happened fast, Salsa Head leaning in and biting the man's nose off, leaving a hole like a fright mask.

Then they were down. On the floor. It didn't take long for the screams to cease.

Carly was now the one dragging. Thom let himself be led to the door, which she opened like a thwarted nightmare. The sun was bright outside. An exact contrast to the black-as-night feeling inside. The teenage thing was shambling behind, neither slow nor stopping.

If they could just get outside, he thought it might not be able to open the door.

Carly threw her shoulder against it, tossing it from ajar to swinging wide.

She fell more than ran outside, Thom stumbling behind her.

But the door didn't close; the thing was barreling behind them.

Suddenly they were in the open air with a monster on their heels. In the sunlight, the thing was even more grotesque. Thom could see it wasn't as whole as he'd imagined. It had scalp trauma, too, and a massive flap hanging behind him atop his hoodie like a second skin — literally, Thom supposed.

He couldn't tell if it was scalp hanging from above or skin from between his shoulders, raised to drape over. The blood, from the rear, was immense. How were they still walking?

Thom's feet betrayed him. His stumble gave way to a fall. Carly's legs caught up with his and then they were on the concrete, the slowly advancing boy now bloodying the ground just a few feet away. It looked hungry — mouth open, teeth bared, with a vacant, ravenous expression.

It was closer.

Closer.

Until something new burst through the just-closed mall doors behind them and ran hard at the monstrosity.

Thom thought it was another of them (a fast one, and now they were *really* in trouble).

But it was his father.

Rick, unlike Thom, had chosen a real weapon — and, also unlike Thom, was prepared to use it.

He held an axe like the one from earlier. The fireman variety: big, long, red, and with a spike on the rear to counterpoint the blade on the front.

Moving like a man thirty years his junior, Rick swung the weapon in a balletic arc. The spike end buried itself in the creature's skull with a crack that sounded like dropped plaster.

All movement instantly stopped.

The thing became a sack of laundry. It fell in a pile, untidy with the axe like a handle for its brain.

Then Rick looked at Thom and Carly, standing over them like an action hero. "Don't you two know anything? You have to hit them in the head."

Ambulatory Corpses

Rick brushed one hand against the other in a

gesture of tidy completion, then reached out for Carly.

As Thom followed her up, he noticed her limp for the first time. They'd been in such a shambling rush to get out of the mall that he hadn't seen. It wasn't big, but enough to throw off her natural stride.

He took her from Rick and walked to a short retaining wall, where they both sat. He noticed with relief that Brendan had made his way around to the Macy's exit as well. Must've been following their dot on the GPS.

Their respite would be short. Thom had to keep reminding himself that they still didn't have Rosie and would need to find her — not eventually, but within minutes. Remembering the remaining task on their collective plate would require constant effort. It was beyond tempting to wait for the ambulances, then let themselves get cared for. Carly could get her ankle taped, and some kind EMT could give Brendan hot chocolate and wrap him in a blanket.

But that fantasy fell apart almost immediately.

Why would EMTs be driving around with hot chocolate?

It always looked so nice when they did it

onscreen. Life could stand to be more like TV sometimes.

He looked at the mall, and the more-or-less empty parking lot into which they'd emerged. The body of the boy-thing, still with the axe in its skull like a high-fashion hat, was facedown between them and the building. Blood pooled all around it, but there didn't seem enough for a cranial axe wound. Head wounds were supposed to bleed like a bitch.

So maybe a little *less* like TV, in this particular case.

With his mind alive with terror and a sense they'd just managed the nearest of misses, Thom made himself breathe more slowly, with a serious attempt at making a return to center. So much had just happened, and all of it so fast. None of it made sense. It would take Thom days to assimilate all he'd seen today, and probably the rest of his life to so much as try and forget it.

Carly winced as she shifted on the wall.

"Did you twist it?" Thom asked.

She shifted and he saw blood. Not a lot, but enough to come through her jeans in a rash of small spots. He reached down and touched the denim. Carly winced again.

"More than twisted," Thom said.

"The guy I mentioned, with the bashed-open scalp? When we first met, he sort of grabbed me."

Thom raised her pant leg. She was wearing those micro-socks that vanish into the shoe. Her ankle showed skin whenever she shifted, and that was where Thom now saw a semicircle of flat, slightly arced wounds.

"Did he bite you?" Rick was standing above them again.

When Thom took Carly to the wall, Rick and Brendan had paired off. They'd been chatting with animation, and all Thom could think (yes, even now) was that they were encouraging each other. Bad influences, the both of them.

"Something did," Carly said.

Rick moved closer. He examined the wounds, then stood with a strange expression. Brendan was watching. Rick noted it, then broke his stillness, waving for Thom and Carly to rise. "Come on. Don't be a wimp."

"Rick, she's—"

"We need to find Rosie, Thom," his father interrupted.

"I know we need to find Rosie," Thom spat back.

"Can you walk okay?" Rick's ears seemed to cock, so Thom cocked his as well.

There were too many sirens. Some were east and some were west, and in each direction Thom thought he might be able to make out two or three separate sources. They were standing on a slightly elevated spot. Down on the road, Thom watched a fire engine and an ambulance pass the building without turning in.

Where were they all headed?

"Yeah. But if someone could bring the car around instead …"

Thom was about to say sure, but Rick was already shaking his head. "We need to stay together."

"I can protect them, Grandpa," Brendan said, coming alongside them. He was getting so tall. Already longer than Carly, and now Thom saw that his son's height was climbing closer to Rick's. "Dad, let me have your pipe."

Thom realized he was still holding the thing, and with some degree of surprise. He remembered doing a lot of things inside that had required at least one hand (opening doors, pushing racks aside) and was pretty sure a few had required two. Like holding Carly's hand *while* opening doors and pushing racks aside.

Was he wrong about that? He wanted to audit his moves action by action, to follow the fencepost's path through recent history. Maybe he'd tucked it under his armpit.

"Dad."

"No, Brendan. You are not playing guardian so your grandfather can play valet."

"He's right, Brendan. Like I said, we stick together."

Rick was on Thom's side, but something about the exchange still managed to snap his final straw. He *just* said no. Why did Rick think he got the final word on where his grandson went and why?

"Where the hell did you go?" Thom demanded, staring at Rick.

"What?"

"Where did you go? You were supposed to be eating yogurt. The three of you. *Sticking together.*"

Rick looked incredulous. "In case you didn't notice, something happened between then and now."

"Oh, please, Rick," Carly said, remembering that she was supposed to be pissed. "You ran off before anything even started! You decided you wanted to run *toward* the commotion rather than away, just like always, and who cares if you promised not to?"

"I don't think I promised that today," Rick said.

"Don't get technical with me."

"You were watching us, Carly. When I got up, I just assumed you'd see it. When you didn't stop us, I assumed it didn't bother you."

"And don't gaslight me, either! You know I didn't see you go, because you didn't just *leave.* You *snuck away!*"

"Is it my fault you weren't paying attention?"

Carly's head tilted from one direction to the other with her shifting expression, moving from listening to scowling, as in *Don't start this shit with me.*

"Okay, okay," said Brendan, their unlikely peacemaker. "Fighting won't change anything."

It was the wrong tactic, only reminding Thom that he was pissed at Brendan as well.

"Fighting won't change anything? Is that why the first thing you did when we saw that crazy woman in the hallway—"

"Which crazy woman?" Rick asked.

"The first one!" Thom snarled, putting such rancor on the words that Rick should, unless he was

stupid, know quite clearly that the answer had no follow-up.

"I was trying to help, Dad!"

"Did I tell you to help? Didn't I tell you it was a job for the guards?"

"Oh, come on, Dad. You saw how much the *guards* helped."

"What does that mean?" Carly asked.

"Nothing," Thom said.

"Don't treat me like a child!" Carly yelled. "I asked you a question!"

"Okay. Okay." Now Rick was the one waving his hands for a ceasefire. "Doesn't matter. Let's all just calm down."

"Calm down?" Carly spat.

"Yes, calm down." Rick sounded more rational and more lucid than he had in years. As if combat was calling the elder out of retirement. "Let's not get all pissy with each other just yet. That comes later." He glanced down at Carly's ankle. "A lot comes later."

"What?"

"A little kindness is in order," Rick continued. "This is *everyone's* first zombie apocalypse."

"Oh, for fuck's sake." Despite what they'd been through and despite the fact that their quest wasn't over yet and they remained one fragile person short, Thom still found a moment to bury his face in his open palms.

Carly shook her head. "Please, Rick … don't start."

But Rick looked incredulous. "Are you kidding me? What needs to happen before you'll believe me?"

"Believe *you?*" Thom said.

"Yes, *me!* How long have I been warning you?"

"Dad …"

"Just … just forget it, Rick," Carly said.

"Do you think this is just people going nuts for shopping? Treating the mall like it's an even Blacker Friday?"

"No, Dad, I think a few sick people …"

"Sick!"

"I believe you, Grandpa," said Brendan, moving closer toward the knot.

"Oh, great." Thom shook his head, exasperated.

"You know what?" Rick took a beat to cast a subversive glance at his son. "Take my axe."

Thom stood and snatched the axe before Rick could hand it to Brendan. He was inches from his father's face, two men staring one another down as if seconds away from the first punch in a bar fight.

"Oh, so you want the axe?" Rick asked. "You want to be a man?"

"What's that mean?" Carly asked.

"It means he's not happy enough that his grandson *went after* one of those things instead of staying back like I told him to," Thom answered. "Your influence, Dad. *Your* doing."

Brendan was insulted. "Hey, that was my choice! Someone was being attacked and I wanted to help!"

Rick slapped him on the back. "Good for you, son. Not enough bravery in the world. Not enough heroes."

"He's fourteen!"

"Damn right — he *is* fourteen!"

"You're not the only one with wisdom here, you know," Thom told his father. "Maybe I've got some, too. Maybe I know a thing or two. Maybe — just maybe — I've gotten along so far in life just fine doing things my way instead of yours."

There was a moment in which Rick seemed like he might attack the premise (perhaps Thom wasn't getting along fine; he might just be wrong about that), but then the argumentative expression left his hard, rough-skinned features. And again he looked at Carly's ankle before returning his attention to Thom.

"This is your chance to step up, son. All the things you backed away from in the past — none of it matters if you have the balls to do the right thing now."

"Oh, for … Okay. What's the right thing, Dad? Why don't you clue me in?"

"Maybe start with facing what's really happening here."

"Which is zombies," Thom said in his let-me-just-get-this-straight voice.

"Ambulatory corpses." Rick offered the group a nod. "Call them whatever you want."

"Zombies aren't real. Nothing you talk about is real. It's all bullshit, Dad. You're living a goddamn fantasy!"

"Thom …"

"He won't face it, Carly! He can't stand the thought of getting old. I don't know what's more tiresome, Dad — your illness, which you can't help but *which you have* whether you want to admit it or not, or the idiotic things you say when you're feeling just fine."

"Such as?"

"Do you know the difference between movies and reality? Do you *really* think there's a monster in your closet, or is that just *you* being nuts like usual?"

"Thom!"

He turned on her. "Make up your mind, Carly! Is he a doddering old man who can't help himself or is he a fully functional, fully coherent ex-Marine who does and says what he wants with full awareness of how fucked up it all is? He can't have it both ways!"

"He's not …" She glanced at Rick, and Thom knew she was trying not to talk behind his back while he stood right in front of them. "That's not how it works."

"Maybe it's you, Thomas," Rick said.

"Me?"

"Maybe *you're* the one who can't think straight. You just watched a bunch of people going totally batshit, and I heard Carly tell you about the guy who was shot in the heart, then got back up and came after you. If you don't like the word 'zombie,' use something else. But you're stupid if you keep refusing to see what this is."

"THIS! IS NOT! A MOVIE!"

Rick's jaw rocked slowly back and forth, his eyes never leaving Thom's. He was either looking for the perfect response or an ideal insult. But instead he spoke in his calmest voice. "Tensions are high, I get it. But we've still got something we need to do here."

"What, build a bunker? Board our windows?"

Rick glared at his son. "Find Rosie."

And Thom was instantly humbled.

Because despite his determination to keep Rosie in mind, he had of course entirely forgotten.

ELEVEN

Not Like Detectives

Thom wanted to re-trace Brendan's steps right away and return to the lower-level exit. *That's* where he said he'd seen Rosie, so *that's* where they'd need to start.

But the unresolved thing in Thom's mind returned immediately after Rick pitched the same idea: Brendan saying "I *saw* Rosie" instead of "I *see* Rosie."

He'd reported an observation, not a rendezvous.

In *past,* not *present,* tense.

That had bugged Thom when he'd heard it, but then the mayhem exploded, and they'd had all of that haunted-house creeping around with his heart lurching up into his throat the whole time, all the blood and death and things Rick kept stubbornly calling zombies. The incongruity of his son's report was front-and-center again, soon as a temporary peace descended and they started to walk.

"I tried to get to her, Grandpa." Because with the divide in their group, Brendan was speaking more to his grandfather than Thom. "But all these people kept coming out, and the doors, there's like ten of them lined up. I was way at one end and she came out of the last or next-to-last door, so I tried to get through the crowd to her, but ... Well, people were really freaking out. And kind of trampling anyone who got in their way. I actually got close enough to yell her name, but there was a big group of frat-boy guys shoving their way between us and I thought if she heard and started to come toward me, they'd just push her down."

"That was smart," Rick said.

And Brendan beamed.

Thom actually thought the same, but he wasn't about to say it now.

"I kept an eye on her. She was just kind of standing there confused, so I thought if I let them pass ..."

"It's okay," said Thom. "You did fine."

Rick shot Thom a look. To Brendan he said, "Then what happened?"

"More people came out. A lot of them. Like, a *ton!* And Grandpa? Dad?" he said, tossing Thom a bone. "They weren't all …" He shrugged. "You know."

"There were zombies in with them?"

"Goddammit, Dad," said Thom, but nobody seemed to hear him.

Brendan nodded. "A lot of shouting and people running everywhere, some of them even into each other. One of them saw me and started coming right after me."

Carly gasped and put a hand over her mouth.

"It was that woman from earlier, Dad. The lady with all the curls. She …" Brendan drew a breath as if to fortify himself. "Remember how you thought that guy got her with the axe right after we went to get the guards? He must have. She had this big 'ol gash right here …" He drew a vertical line down the center of his chest. "And there was …" A small but involuntary recoil. "I think there was bone sticking out and all this gross stuff kind of dripping from … I could *see inside her.*"

"You have to kill the brain," Rick said. "Otherwise they get right back up."

"You don't know that." Carly turned to her son and added, "He doesn't know that."

Rick seemed to consider a rebuttal, but then seemed to decide that peace — for the sake of finding his girlfriend — mattered more. "Did you see where Rosie went?"

Brendan nodded, half-ashamed. "Yeah. There were a bunch of those cops with these weird silver guns. They were waving people over as they came out of the mall."

"Silver guns?" Rick asked.

"Go on, Brendan," Carly prompted.

"What cops? Who carries silver guns?"

"It's not important," she told Rick.

"Service pistols are almost always black. I think Bakersfield PD carries a Glock 22. It's—"

"Not important," Carly said again.

"Wait," Thom said. "I saw something like that earlier. Did the guns have belled ends?"

Brendan nodded.

"Belled ends?" Rick said.

"Rick," Carly said. Meaning: *Stop interrupting.*

"No, no, that means something," Thom said, reluctant to agree with his father. "I saw two people running through the Macy's looking like Men in Black. Suits and ties, but they didn't seem like detectives."

"But the weapons …" Rick said.

"They looked like muskets. And …" His mind replayed the thing's firing, the way it had whistled instead of banged, and how instead of making a hole in its target, it'd lifted an entire clothing rack in the air and twisted the thing like a pretzel. "And I wouldn't want to be in front of one when someone pulled the trigger."

"What happened after the cops rounded people up?" Carly asked.

"Dunno. People didn't stop coming out, and there were more and more of those crazy people in with them."

"Zombies," Rick clarified.

"I couldn't get to her. I couldn't even see her after a while!" Brendan looked like he might be starting to lose control. All their recent trauma combined with his own failed task hitting him at once, and a sweet woman's whereabouts unknown — because of him, he seemed to feel. "I think they took them. Back the way we came, Dad. Like behind the Halloween Store?"

The Halloween Store. Another forgotten oddity came into his mind. "You mean where all those Hemisphere vans were?"

Brendan nodded.

"What vans?" Rick asked.

"We saw a group of vans when we came around the mall," Thom explained. "All by themselves in a small lot behind the old JC Penney. They had *Hemisphere* written on the side. They—"

But Rick was already running.

TWELVE

Hemisphere

THE OLD MAN had no trace of his ancient injuries.

No arthritis, no stiff joints, no being-68-years-old at all.

Trying to keep pace and failing, Thom got the distinct sense of having traveled back in time. He wasn't chasing his elderly, resident-home father. Instead, he was in pursuit of the hulking Marine Rick had once been — twenty-five years old at most, and aching for action.

By the time Thom caught up with him, huffing and puffing, Rick's breath was mostly back to normal. They stood side-by-side at the edge of the utility lot, and only after finding it empty did Thom remember he'd left his charges behind.

"Is this where you saw them?" Rick asked.

Thom nodded so he'd have another second to find his breath. "Yeah."

"You're sure?"

"I'm sure. We've pretty much made the whole circuit now. This is the only lot like this."

Rick moved forward as Brendan and Carly reached the slope behind them and started scrambling up. Carly wasn't as fast as she usually was with her injury, but Brendan was clearly being the dutiful son, staying with her instead of rushing ahead like Thom had.

At first, still caught in the delusion of his father as Young-Rick-from-the-past, Thom half-thought he planned to kneel and scan the ground for signs like a Native American tracker. Instead, he reached the spot where the vans had been parked, made a slow rotation, then came halfway back. He heard Carly huffing and puffing up the slope and waved Thom forward.

"Look. I know you don't like me much right now."

"Right now," Thom echoed.

"But before they get up here, there's something you need to understand."

"Okay."

"It's about Carly."

"Okay."

"And I think you already know."

Thom looked back. He honestly didn't.

"Her injury," Rick said.

"What about it?"

"She was bitten."

"Okay. And?" Then he understood. "Oh, for fuck's sake, Dad."

"Listen. This is important. I know you don't believe me."

"No, Dad, I don't."

"And when I say how I know what I'm about to tell you, you're going to believe me even less."

"Then why tell me, Dad." He said it like a proof's conclusion, not like a question. It was a statement — a *tout fini* to their entire struggle. They weren't going to agree, so why argue? Why not let it go, and just agree to disagree? Like the WOPR said in *WarGames*, the only winning move was not to play.

"Ever since they started me on that drug — BioFuse — it's like I'm seeing more and more. I can—"

"Seriously?"

But Rick was done being polite; Carly and Brendan were halfway up so they only had seconds. He cut Thom off with a firm, unapologetic hand, and delivered his next line like a drill sergeant.

"Goddammit, listen to me! You're going to think I'm full of shit right now, but I want you to know this when things get worse, which they absolutely will, so you can start getting it through your thick skull."

Thom wanted to snap at that (if either of them had a thick skull, it was Rick), but he, like Brendan, still had some fatherly obedience baked in.

"Don't interrupt. Let me talk. If you want to take me back and declare me nuts, that's your business. Just hear me. You got that?"

Thom nodded.

Rick glanced past his son one last time, then spoke in a rush. "My brain has changed. Like … it's stronger now, but in weird ways. I know things I don't really think I have any way of knowing."

"Like the monster in your closet."

Rick gave Thom a death stare, and Thom resolved to do as he was told from here on out, and not interrupt.

"I think this is happening all over town. I don't know why. It's … in here," he explained, pressing his temples. "Carly's been bitten. Even you must know, deep down, that it's a problem, even if this is just Rip Daddy."

That was true, but Rip Daddy didn't spread fast and there was an existing treatment. They just couldn't get to all the new cases in time.

"She's going to become like them eventually. I don't know why it's not happening already. Maybe it's faster when they take bigger bites; I've really got no idea. The only way I can explain it to you is … I just know I'm right."

Thom didn't respond. *I just know I'm right* was the battle cry of every delusion ever known.

"We have to watch her, Thom. Don't let her get too close to any of us, especially if she starts to get foggy or not-all-there."

"You don't want to kill her outright? Isn't that what people do when they're bitten by zombies?"

"I want to try something first." Thom didn't like his qualifier: *first*. "You said the vans here were Hemisphere vehicles."

"Yeah."

"And they took Rosie."

"Maybe."

"Probably."

"Oh yeah? Why?"

"Because Rosie was with us. And I think they were looking for me."

Great. Delusions of grandeur atop everything. "Five vans, Dad. The Big Bad Company took *five vans* ... to come after *you*."

"Not just me. But I was on their list for sure."

"Why?"

"Why what?" Brendan asked, finally arriving with his mother in tow.

Thom gave her a glance, hating Rick for the fresh doubt he'd put into his mind. His wife was even whiter than usual, like she'd been drained of blood. That made sense; she'd been through a panic and had just overexerted herself with a bum leg.

But now Thom also saw something sinister. Something impossible that he still couldn't entirely ignore. Rick had been right about just hearing him out without comment. He knew the information would settle inside his son's orderly, no-loose-ends mind and make its home there.

Now, he'd never be able to get rid of it.

Rick gave Thom a look: *Don't forget what we talked about.*

Then he took a breath and switched to family-safe mode. "I was just telling your dad that these were Hemisphere vans, and that Hemisphere has me on a list."

Thom looked at Carly for help, but she was simply listening, same as Brendan. Seeing their expressions made him feel alone. No longer in the majority, two-thirds of his family had been sucked into Rick's delusions.

"Why?" Brendan asked.

"I'm not sure. I just know the trial I'm in has been strange lately. They're supposed to send a nurse once a week. She comes to my room, asks me a few questions about my mood, then tests me with flash cards, like to see if I can remember them. Sometimes I get a little medical exam. And they draw blood every time. They give me another shot of BioFuse at the end, then they thank me and leave. Always polite. Always the same old routine. But the past few times, they've sent someone with the nurse. Doesn't look like a doctor, though. He always wears a black suit with a skinny black tie."

That made Thom blink. If it was fantasy, Rick had spun it beautifully.

"Now there are always extra tests. Sometimes I'm asked what's on flash cards they haven't shown me yet. At first I thought it was a mistake, but then the nurse did the same thing again and again. They don't just draw blood now, either. Once they explained that I would have to go under. It was one of my fuzzier days so I suppose I agreed. I woke up with my leg aching and little Band-Aids on my thigh and forehead. I think they might have taken samples from my brain."

"Out of your *leg?*" Brendan asked.

"I think that might have been marrow. I think I somehow heard them talking in my sleep."

Thom laughed.

"Quiet, Thom," said Carly.

"And now Hemisphere's here," Rick continued, oblivious to the ill looks exchanged between man and wife. "They're at the mall, right when this happens. And what do they do? They round up folks coming out, pick some to take with them, and scatter the rest."

"*They* scattered. You don't know that Hemisphere—"

Carly raised her eyebrows at Thom, so he stopped.

Rick said, "I know what I did in there was stupid, but I also think it saved my ass. I wanted to see what was going on because I was tired of being babysat, so I told Rosie we'd go shopping and we sneaked away when Carly wasn't paying attention.

But when we got to the top of the escalator, I looked back and saw four of your Men in Black back where we'd just been sitting, wearing silver guns with belled ends."

Thom rolled his head back. "Oh, bull*shit!* You're just repeating back what I said!"

"Dad," Brendan said. "Maybe we should listen."

"They kept their coats closed, but a few had them unbuttoned so whenever they swung around, I could see the weapons. And I'm sure that they were looking for me."

"Of course you are," Thom said. "Because you're paranoid."

But even he was starting to wish he'd shut up because evidence of blossomed paranoia was right in front of them in the form of five departed vans. Even Thom had thought the vehicles were suspicious when he and Brendan had come through.

"Maybe, but here's what I know," Rick said, his tone already less confrontational as he won allies. "Rosie's not exactly a sprinter. The fastest I've seen her move is when the cafeteria has green Jell-O, and it's a mild shuffle at best. We were inside a while, then behind Macy's, where nobody else was coming out. So, okay, people ran off. But Brendan says

Rosie went with the suit guys. Are we supposed to believe that she broke free, then hauled ass? If for some reason she *did* decide to run away, I'm pretty sure we'd still be able to see her. At the very least, Brendan would have, once he escaped all the mayhem."

He took a breath, then continued. "I also know that if she didn't run away on foot, she couldn't have taken your car because she doesn't drive, and even if she did, the two of you had the keys. And I'm also pretty sure she doesn't know how to hotwire a random vehicle. So, what's left?"

"The vans," said Carly.

"Whether you believe me or not—" Rick gave his son an earnest look. "—the trail to finding Rosie starts with Hemisphere."

Two new sirens screamed in the distance. It suddenly struck Thom how quiet and still it was up here *other* than the sirens, which were multiplying by the moment.

Shouldn't there be cars circling to park?

Shouldn't there be new arrivals to the mall, getting out of their cars before sensing something amiss?

The place had been packed, and yet there wasn't a single straggler around right now. No matter how Thom sliced it — even denying everything his father said — things were rotting in Denmark.

"I guess I can go get the car," Thom said.

"No way," Brendan told him, looking at their foursome. "This time, we all go."

THIRTEEN

Guile

Thom's doubts sloughed away like dead skin the minute they left the mall's orbit.

The complex was a rough circle, with twin paths circling the ring of parking lots. You had to turn onto the outer road, then take a short access road to reach the boulevard beyond. The entire way was clear, and that was unusual — but what lay out in the wider world was even more surprising.

Pure chaos. The second they drove into it, Thom wished they'd stayed at the mall. He hadn't realized how good they'd momentarily had it. Other than the one creature who'd chased Thom and Carly through an open door, no others seemed to have emerged. With the doors closed, they might as well have been locked.

In the quiet parking lot with all the people gone, the somewhat-higher-than-its-surroundings mall had been like a citadel during a storm. Now they were in the soup at its base, and it wasn't the everyday calm he'd expected.

Cars had crashed, and no emergency vehicles attended them. Injured people were everywhere, shambling along vacant-eyed and with zero direction. But when Thom stopped to help one of them, it reached through the window and nearly clawed his face off.

They passed by others in the same condition, this time with all the windows up, and got the same result. They were surrounded whenever they stopped. To break the tension, Brendan told his dad to go ahead and let them wash the windshield. Thom tried to laugh, but funny might be dead for a while.

Sirens were everywhere, but they were always moving, never seeming to stop. Some of those on foot around them kept attacking others, usually in an animal frenzy from which Carly tried, without success, to hide Brendan's eyes.

They drove past a park centered with a beautiful gazebo, but the structure had been knocked askew, and there was a red mass slumped against one interior wall that Thom sincerely hoped wasn't human but of course almost certainly was.

"Look," Brendan said, leaning his head against the window and looking up. "Helicopters."

Thom craned to see, but immediately realized that he didn't have to.

There were more of them through the windshield, and their presence wasn't subtle. They were low, and they were large — the kind that ferried troops and had massive guns.

Thom nearly caused a collision while staring up at the sky.

Carly screamed for him to look out; a city bus was barreling down a wreck-littered throughway and, as they all watched, T-boned an SUV driving perpendicular.

Thom repeatedly tried turning onto larger roads, but the widest ones were gridlocked. Pedestrians walked between cars, visible from the surface roads, but Thom doubted they were everyday folks who'd run out of gas. Hints he saw while trying to keep his eyes fixed to the road — combined with small disturbed noises from Carly, Brendan, and even Rick — suggested the walkers were pulling others from their cars, then using them for a meal.

"LOOK OUT!"

No time. Thom registered Carly's shout a half-second after she verbalized it, then yanked the wheel a half-second after that. But the two slumping forms had come from nowhere. Thom, who'd pressed the gas nearly to the floor without realizing (and driving more often than not on sidewalks and berms) had no time to avoid them.

He saw their faces before plowing into them, noting them as vacant, and knowing them to be like the others. One went under the car and another struck the windshield. It was like they'd decided to divide and conquer, except that Thom's Volvo was the one concluding their encounter in triumph.

The thing that'd gone over the car had left a lot of its skull behind and stayed down, but the one Thom ran over did not. His speed and a lucky strike had severed the woman nearly in half, but when Thom glanced in his rearview, he saw her take the hit, turn in a crawl, and keep on coming with guts in long red ropes behind her.

They found a street that wasn't clotted and swung a hard right, but a single glimpse of a tank and a handful of National Guard vehicles turned him right back around.

Past the vehicles, he'd spied not just orange-and-white traffic barricades, but four-point tank-stoppers strung with razor wire.

Carly watched it longer than Thom did, revolving fully to look out the rear as they drove back away.

"Turn on the radio," she said.

"I'm not really in the mood," Thom told her.

She reached for the radio and on came the news station.

Thom felt dumb. Again.

A report spilled from a reporter's lips. "—of the unknown outbreak, but thanks to an emergency barricade, News 11 is being assured by both local and national authorities that for now the infection is contained. We're also being told that airspace around Bakersfield has been commandeered by the National Guard and U.S. Army and that the area is considered a *no-fly zone.*"

The reporter said it carefully, as if the words might not be self-evident. "We can't provide you with our own aerial footage, but listeners wishing to view what there is to see of Bakersfield from above can visit our website at News11.org for footage courtesy of the Army. Viewer warning: *What you see there … is disturbing.*"

"Jesus," Thom said. "It must be the whole city."

Rick grunted. "Look on the bright side. At least it's *only* the city."

"Are they saying what it is? Like, what caused it?"

"We all have exactly as much information as you, Thom," said Carly, annoyed.

"But you're still listening."

She was, with the volume lowered. It'd been ten seconds. She glared at him.

"Oh, shit."

"Brendan!" Carly snapped.

No response from Rick, but if that exclamation had come from Thom, Rick would probably be calling him a pussy right about now.

In the mirror, Thom saw a shuffle in the back seat, presumably as Brendan's phone (although, it was actually still *Thom's*) moved from grandson to grandfather. Rick began to scroll, holding the phone high with his left hand and using an arthritis-gnarled finger to move down the page.

He tapped, and Thom watched their heads lean close to watch a video.

Thom, up front, could only hear snarls. What sounded like jackals feeding.

Now, still in the mirror, Brendan was paper-white.

To his credit, Rick snatched the phone, still looking, but no keeping the screen away from his grandson. "Service sucks. I guess we're lucky the mall stayed lit, because this says power's going out all over the city. You wanna know why?"

"No," said Carly.

"They've got us all blocked in, but the power plant's in with us. And ..."

"The nuclear plant?" Thom asked.

"No. Luckily. The coal one. Anyone know which plant powers which areas? I'd rather not be in the dark when night comes."

"Wait," Brendan said. "We can't leave? We're staying here tonight?"

Rick either didn't hear or didn't care to answer. "Says here most of the cell towers are down, and the coal plant supplied power to most of the providers, so it's moot anyway. The signal I'm getting is probably coming from somewhere beyond the barricade."

"Should I stay out near the edges, so we can get a signal?"

"No. We have to head toward downtown."

"Downtown?" Thom said it like a swear. Rick's proposal was tantamount to going down into a

spooky basement while ghosts prowled the neighborhood, or teenagers doing it in a tent with a serial killer on the loose. "We need to get out. No way we're going downtown!"

"What about our home?" Carly asked.

"According to this," Rick read from the phone, "your neighborhood is about the worst place in the world we could possibly go. Seems a helicopter went down." He looked through all the windows, then pointed. Thom saw a rising line of smoke in the distance. "There. And it ..."

"It what?"

"It kind of ... rang the dinner bell."

"Where are they all coming from?"

"From the population." Rick shrugged. "Zombie apocalypses are a sort of self-sustaining situation."

Thom wanted to shout or laugh at the mention again of "zombies," but he couldn't summon the breath. If it walked like a duck and quacked like a duck, Thom was very unfortunately starting to think maybe it wasn't his business to keep insisting that it wasn't a duck.

"You're saying the zombies create more zombies?" Brendan said.

"Basically, yeah."

"Because, like, when someone gets bit?"

Rick shrugged.

"Mom?" Brendan said, eyes ticking in the general direction of her ankle wound.

"Why downtown, Dad?" Thom rushed to change the subject.

"That's where Hemisphere is."

"We're so not going to Hemisphere anymore," Thom said.

"Yes we are," Rick insisted.

"No, we're not."

"What about Rosie?"

"What *about* Rosie?" Thom asked.

"You signed her out. She's your responsibility."

"We didn't sign her out. Her daughter signed her out."

"Seriously, Thomas? You're an asshole."

"Let it go, Dad."

"An asshole and a coward."

"Whatever. I just want to survive."

"Like a coward asshole."

"Language!" Carly had sweat on her brow. Thom tried not to see it.

Rick leaned forward, putting a forearm on each front seat. "I know you don't think you're going to drive through a military barricade."

"No, I was going to find a safe place, inside Bakersfield, to ride it out."

"Ride what out?" Rick waved his arms all around. "This right here? It's already ridden. You're good at math, son. What do you call it when one makes two, and two make four, and four make eight?"

"You don't know that's how it is."

"I goddamn well do, and only half of it are the reasons you know."

Thom considered balking, but he was no longer poised to rebut anything his father told him.

"So what do you call it?" Rick pressed.

Begrudgingly, Thom said, "Exponential."

"So you know how fast this is going to slide out of control. Shit. It's *already* out of control. And it's only gonna get worse. We aren't going to your home or that dungeon where you've stuck me, because they're both in the middle of what the news says is a mass buffet. You can't get us out. So, okay, you want to lay low. Where? And here's the most important question: *For how long?*"

"Until it's handled."

Rick laughed. "They've got one city that's a problem, and it's quickly becoming a *very serious one.* From what I see, it's only us. Only Bakersfield. So what would *you* do, if you were the military lead in charge of 'handling' this? Does the word *triage* mean anything to you? How about *acceptable losses*?"

"Dad?" Brendan pleaded.

Rick gave the boy a glance, then said somewhat quieter, "Listen to me, Thom. You didn't believe anything else I said, but maybe you're willing to hear me now. *You can't wait this out.*" He took another look at Brendan, then seemed to decide that the truth needed to be said, no matter how scary it might be. "I know what I'd do, and it wouldn't be opening the gates and trying to sort us out one by one. I don't know what happened here any more than you do, but I do know that Hemisphere is somehow caught up in it, and that 'laying low' and hoping they let us out later is only gonna get us all dead. So, there's really only one choice left."

"What's that?"

"Guile."

The car was silent.

"What's that mean?" Brendan asked.

"Cunning," Rick clarified. "Cleverness. Coercion. It means we need to use our brains, if we don't want to see them get eaten."

"But … What's it *mean?*"

Carly answered, having assembled his puzzle fastest.

"It means," she told her son, "that we're going to Hemisphere."

FOURTEEN

Exponential Growth

THEIR LUCK with the car didn't hold out.

The mall was on the outskirts, near the edge of the city-wide blockade, and as near as Thom could tell, it had either been the incident's epicenter or one of several that happened at the same time.

If his father had theories about how it'd all gone down, Thom was finally ready to welcome them. But Rick was silent and Thom refused to humble himself enough to ask, so by the time he hit an impassable wreck, he'd decided it ultimately didn't matter.

What did matter was how *fast* everything had gone down — a supernatural speed to accompany what should have been a supernatural disease.

Everything had been fine when they'd left for the mall.

It seemed like the nightmare had happened within the last … What? Two hours?

There hadn't been a slow rotting of Bakersfield. This whole thing had dropped like a rock into a pond.

And that, thought Thom as he carefully parked the car and pocketed the keys just in case they'd return to it, was only the tip of things. For the rest of the decent part of the drive, his passengers had been quiet. Without taking a census, Thom thought that Brendan was scared for his life, his future, and his mother; Carly in turn feared for Brendan and her worsening bite; Rick was devouring all the news he could and (if Past Rick was any indication) probably formulating a plan.

Thom had been thinking in the quiet. About the suddenness of the change, but also about the almost immediate response. By all reports, the Bakersfield blockade was military atop military, and it wasn't like all those tanks and troops had just been sitting around, taking in the sun and shopping at Vons.

How had they dropped that hammer so fast?

And he thought of Hemisphere. To Thom, the

company was only an academic construct, not something he'd really ever had intimate knowledge of. He knew it as a drug company with a charismatic but obnoxious founder, and as the manufacturer of BioFuse. He'd never heard of the drug before the home's resident liaison called to ask for a bit of Thom and Carly's time to discuss a potential Alzheimer's trial.

Thom had been skeptical about the trial because that was his nature. Carly was skeptical because she worked in medicine and had seen vain attempts to slay the Alzheimer's dragon before. Rick wasn't skeptical at all. He was losing his mind. And life, per Rick, would be pointless without it.

Fry my brain, liquify it in my skull — I really don't care, if there's a chance you can fix me, too.

Because Thom was his guardian at the time (still was, but he'd *needed* a guardian then and even Rick could admit it), his consent mattered most. So Thom had researched, talked contentiously to Rick when his father was lucid, reviewed all Hemisphere could give him on the drug, and even spoke to a biochemist he knew from college.

Not every light had been green, but enough were in the family for Thom to finally agree to the experimental trial. Two weeks later Rick had taken his baseline tests and been given his first dose of BioFuse using a small, aesthetically unobjectionable injection device the company simply called a "gadget." The next week, another. Then another. It took about a month for Rick to show any improvement, and Thom knew he was getting better because Thom started hating him a whole lot more. Ironically, a sick father was a big improvement over a healthier one. Turned out the trial was really a choice between Rick's well-being and his son's.

With the treatments working so well, Thom had mostly stopped asking questions. BioFuse became one thing while, quite separately, wider Hemisphere became something else. Founder Archibald Burgess had started appearing on a growing number of magazine covers, while other drugs in the company's suite gained popular (if mysterious) favor.

Hemisphere had a way of generating more rumor than fact, and that was strange for a company that required so much paperwork and compliance to function. Whispers abounded about drugs that could make people live longer, feel a lot better, and look like models even if they'd been near the soil of an ugly tree. Nobody could substantiate or prove those rumors, but the internet swore they were true. True, and also not technically by-the-books as far as the FDA was concerned.

The company's infamy grew alongside its fame.

All these things, Thom had thought about Hemisphere. But it really wasn't like that, because while Thom had indeed had all the thoughts, they were only in passing. He didn't obsess about the company. He didn't think the pharmaceutical enterprise was God's Greatest Gift or the Devil. He noticed Archibald Burgess in the news but didn't stalk him or seek any information beyond what naturally came his way, and even though his father was benefitting from Burgess's invention, Thom only had tolerance for a few hours a month spent thinking about his old man.

And so it had stayed in the background like ambient music: always there, never truly a presence.

Until now.

Now, Thom wished he'd paid more attention. The closer they came to the city's center, the worse their cell reception became. A few miles before they had to pull over and walk, Rick announced his surrender. There was really no new news to be found about Hemisphere for the Shelton family. Thom had only his memories, and for once he hadn't obsessed or worried enough.

Because, what was Hemisphere relative to all of this?

Rick seemed to know more than he was saying, but Thom was afraid to ask why for more than the usual reasons. Namely, because his father had sort of already told them where some of his information was coming from, and Thom didn't want to believe it.

So far, most if not all of Rick's tall tales had proven to be true. There probably *had* been vans following them on the way to the mall, there really *were* horror movie monsters in the world, the doctors *might have* given Rick special, top-secret treatment in his trial, and apparently Rick had seen it all coming.

If his father was somehow psychic as well (the drug worked on the brain and Hemisphere's slogan was *Upgrading Nature,* after all), Thom didn't want to know. Rick was bad enough outside his head without the risk of him being inside it as well.

The coincidences were too big to ignore. But, as they walked, Thom put a silver lining on that particular cloud. If he was forced to accept that Rick's conspiracy theories might be more truth than Alzheimer's Disease, it at least gave them a lead to follow. It was bizarre (and troubling) to think that his father's pharma sponsors might be somehow involved in this, but at least believing it gave them all a goal and something to do.

A desperate sort of hope had infiltrated the group, but desperate hope that Hemisphere had the answers was better than no hope at all.

"I wish we had guns," Brendan said as they crouched behind a wreck. Black and smoking, warm but not hot to the touch, with everyone pretending there wasn't a charred body still sitting in the cab.

"No you don't," said Thom.

"Yes I do."

"Then I guess I don't." Carly looked like wax, the off-yellow of recycled paper. She was limping more now, and the last time Thom had checked on her ankle, he'd hoped to never see it again. Her skin looked like meat left in the sun — the kind of thing you cut away because it couldn't be saved.

Brendan seemed about to rebut again, but one look at his mother closed his mouth. Her words had the feeling of a dying wish, and he damn well knew it.

"How are you feeling, Carly?" Rick asked with surprising tenderness.

"I've been better."

"Can you go on?"

"I will. I'm not fond of the alternative."

Thom wasn't sure which alternative she meant. Did she mean dying? Did she mean holing up alone, waiting out the boys' excursion until they returned, dodging the looters and shooters and biters filling the streets? Or did she mean the third thing — the one that shouldn't be possible, but then again monsters that didn't fall when you cut them in half weren't supposed to be possible, either.

Thom didn't believe in zombies even now; in his mind he kept using "biters" because even kittens could use their teeth. But whatever he called them, the multiplying monsters around them were doing all those traditional zombie things.

They didn't die unless you destroyed their brains; they shambled mindlessly; they formed groups and came on like a very patient army. If those things were actually true, then what Thom didn't want to consider involving Carly was likely true, too. He had no idea why she hadn't turned yet, since so many others seemed to be doing that quickly, but mostly it was just one more thing he needed to ignore.

Nothing they could do, anyway, other than keep on moving.

"How much farther is it?" Brendan asked.

"I've still got their webpage up," Rick answered, looking at Thom's phone. "I think it's in that Minute Clinic that closed, by the Provisions. So maybe a mile or two?"

Something exploded in the right. Not a big blast — more like the crash-whoosh of a Molotov cocktail. Zombie warfare at its finest … but where were all the chainsaws?

They could see a crowd in the direction they needed to go. Whether it was more creatures or normal folks on a rampage, Thom didn't have a clue. He only knew that neither was good.

"Look." Carly was pointing at a line of scooters.

"We need to download an app if we want to use them." Thom held out his hand and waited for his phone. Once he had it back he tried clicking over to the app store, but now his phone wouldn't connect. He held it high, then looked again at the screen. "There isn't any signal."

"Maybe it's just Verizon," Carly said.

He fished out Brendan's borrowed phone, which for some ancient forgotten reason they hadn't bundled into the family plan. Brendan used AT&T, and yes … he had one bar. "I doubt we'll be able to download the app on one bar, though."

Brendan rolled his head back and forth, deciding whether to say something. "Well …"

"What?"

"I sort of already have the app," he admitted.

"Why?" Thom asked.

"I … sort of used one once when I was with Melissa."

His blood boiled. One more way his son hadn't listened. Thom hated the urban scooters. He'd heard too many stories of injuries and deaths, and Carly had seen them firsthand at her hospital.

"Brendan, I told you and told you—"

"Knock it off, Thom. We're lucky the kid's got stones." Rick snatched the phone while Thom resisted another urge to shout at his father for corrupting his son. But no, this very much wasn't the time.

"Here," he said, returning the phone to Brendan. "Show us how."

He not only knew how, Brendan even had a way to activate more than one scooter at a time. One service bar was apparently just enough to activate the scooters, and a few minutes later Thom was blowing through the breeze, for some reason not nearly as scared of the zippy little things as he'd been before.

He took the rear, with Rick at the front and Carly and Brendan sharing a ride in the middle. Carly pretended it was so she could help her son and keep him safe, but really it was the other way around.

Thanks to fancy maneuvering and a lot of luck, making it to Hemisphere wasn't difficult. The scant news they could still get on Brendan's phone (plus plain old observation) suggested that much of the population was moving away from the center toward the edges. Normal people were doing it to escape and getting rebuffed decisively by troops at the border, while the monster things seemed to be following the normals. Reports were fuzzy on how many there were of each. They'd spotted at least twenty of the diseased walkers on their ride downtown, and Thom found himself thinking of what Rick had insisted was happening earlier.

Exponential growth.

Because one turned two or three, then those two or three turned two or three each, and so on until the entire city was dinner. But that only worked with a short generation time — and given the recency of what had happened, it seemed to suggest that the normal generation time was brief indeed. They'd yet to see one turn and rage immediately after getting bitten, but that reality couldn't be too far away.

Carly was, so far, the exception. Because Thom didn't know why, he couldn't relax.

Could it happen in the next five minutes?

Might it never happen at all?

They found the Hemisphere building surrounded — not by people, but by a battalion of army trucks. Their own vans were inside. Another circle, same as they'd seen in the parking lot. There was no way to know if the white vans were the same ones that Thom had seen at the mall.

Thom said as much out loud.

"Maybe, maybe not. But she's here as easily as anywhere else."

Thom stopped himself from asking Rick who he was talking about. He'd forgotten Rosie again, this time in the mad rush to comprehend the impossible and keep on living, seeing this place as the beginning of a way out, maybe, rather than a place of rescue.

He kept his mouth shut and nodded, trying to project solidarity.

"Okay," Carly said. They all looked closer. They were at a distance, but near enough to see that razor wire had been strung between, over, and around the army trucks, effectively freezing them in place among the world's unfriendliest jungle gym. A line of camouflage-attired men and women with machine guns stood behind the wire. "But how are we supposed to get in?"

Thom was wondering if it was even worth trying. They'd come here on a lark, but the chance that a way out lay inside, now that they were here and saw how forbidding it all looked, suddenly seemed unlikely enough to feel foolish. Even if they could get inside, what were they planning to do? Ask nicely for Rosie back (if she was even in the place), then request a Golden Ticket to get them beyond borders that had been thoroughly closed?

He stopped wondering when footsteps sounded behind them.

They turned to see another two soldiers with helmets and long black weapons … plus one of those sliver things on the opposite hip.

"Are you Richard Shelton?" one of them asked.

Rick, surprised at last, nodded.

"Come with us," the other said.

FIFTEEN

Stubborn

THEY FLANKED RICK, more like escorts than captors.

He rose and went without question — probably because dying by machine gun sounded preferable to becoming someone's meal, and because even though the way it'd happened was different than they'd figured, Rick had already sworn to go inside one way or another.

A few steps on, Thom, still hesitating as if nothing had happened, looked at Carly and then at Brendan. Carly shrugged. Brendan said, "Come on, Dad, live a little." It wasn't entirely appropriate to the situation, but it did get Thom to stand ahead of his son. It at least gave him the dignity of following

Rick directly ahead of Brendan, instead of trailing behind.

At a gate they'd built in the barbed wire, Thom thought the two soldiers with Rick might turn, see that they had company, and shoo the rest of the family away — possibly with prejudice. Instead, the first of them nodded at Thom and held the gate open for him. Thom, perplexed, could only say thanks. Carly and Brendan entered behind him, and only then did they close it.

They were greeted by a skeleton crew. There seemed to be only three staffers in the entire place, presumably because the others had found a way to evacuate. Maybe there were more in the back rooms, but the building had been hooked to a generator outside and only one of the back rooms was lit. Rick was right; this had once been a Minute Clinic. It was a fairly large building for just three people, but a couple dozen troops covering the walls like paper made up for it. Or, maybe, they turned it even eerier.

A dark-skinned man with salt-and-pepper hair walked right toward Rick and extended his hand. Rick, looking more lost than he ever had in the depths of his disease, shook it.

"I'm Doctor Sanjay Dhar. I'm second in charge

here." Brendan looked around and Sanjay laughed. "*First* in charge right now," he clarified.

"Rick Shelton."

"Oh, I know," said the doctor. "We've been looking for you."

"What? Why?"

Sanjay didn't seem to hear him. He went to Carly, then Thom, then even to Brendan with an offered hand and a strangely formal hello. He was friendly like a pediatrician. It seemed so completely out of place with all the gunshots popping beyond the walls and the entire city on its way to ruins.

Once finished with introductions, Sanjay took a half second to smile at them.

Long enough for Rick to speak. "What the fuck is going on here?"

Sanjay said, "Oh my. Yes. Right to business. But that fits your tendency, doesn't it?"

"What do you mean?"

"Well, you are hard-charging. 'No BS,' as it were. You accumulated quite the disciplinary record during your time in the Marines and yet you were never held back from advancement, discharging highly decorated. To what do you attribute that?'

Rick made a face that was half incredulous, half scowl.

"Yes. Well," Sanjay said. "I suspect it's neither here nor there. How are you feeling?"

"I'm sorry," Thom interrupted. "Do you have any idea what's happening outside?"

"Oh my, yes," he replied, as if Thom meant a parade instead of an apocalypse. "We've had a bit of a spontaneous, unplanned experiment. Now our challenge is to solve it, but I appreciate a challenge. Do you appreciate a challenge, young man?"

Brendan was so confused, he didn't answer in the doctor's allotted time.

Sanjay smiled as if he had.

"Do you have my Rosie?" Rick asked.

"Pardon?"

"Rose Georgia Sandoval. My grandson said your people rounded up a bunch of folks at the mall. Threw them into vans like you have outside. She was one of them."

It was still a leap. They only knew that Brendan had seen unknown people herding mallgoers toward where the white vans had been parked, and Rick's tone was clearly one of accusation.

Still, Sanjay smiled as if he'd borrowed a pencil and forgotten to give it back. "Oh. Yes. She is in back, resting comfortably."

That sounded medical.

"What did you do to her?" Thom asked.

"Nothing, Mr. Shelton. Why would anything be done to her? To any of them?"

"The others are here, too?"

"Yes, of course. We couldn't just put them out on the street. Bakersfield is not exactly alive with the sound of music. I've been telling my new Army friends that the streets are thriving with the sound of regenerative necrosis … but honestly, I don't think they get it."

"I don't get it," Brendan said.

"Are we prisoners?" Rick asked.

"Prisoners?" A laugh. "Oh my, no. You are one of our valued subjects, and it's my sincere hope that you'll be willing to help us in ways far more beneficial than our original agreement."

Thom wondered what would happen if Rick didn't want to help. The two other medical types in the room looked like assistants, maybe nurses, but there was also a lot of coercive power within the building's walls in the form of automatic weapons and muscle.

"Help how?" Rick asked.

"Oh, I'd just like a sample of your blood."

"You've taken gallons of my blood."

"Yes, but something curious happened lately

and I'd like to know how your body is responding. Or more accurately, I'd like to know why your body *doesn't* appear to be responding at all."

"Does this have something to do with my drug trial?"

Sanjay looked to a man in blue scrubs. The man shook his head. So, not an assistant after all. Probably quietly in charge no matter what the doctor claimed.

"Not at all," he said.

But Thom thought, *That's a lie.*

"What's your role in this, then? Why are you blocked in? Why are there all these soldiers inside to protect you, and a generator to keep the building running, if it all has nothing to do with you?"

"It *currently* has nothing to do with Hemisphere." Sanjay looked again to the other man, who nodded. "It is our sincere hope that we may soon have *everything* to do with it."

"I don't understand," said Carly.

"No, I guess you wouldn't. Would you care to take a seat?"

With no better ideas, they all did.

"Anything to drink? We have soda. I even plugged the coffeemaker into the generator cord; don't tell anyone!"

"No, thanks," said Thom.

Rick shook his head, but Carly and Brendan asked for water.

As the man in scrubs brought the drinks, Sanjay sat down opposite them. Thom felt like they were all in the center ring of a circus. It was as if the building had been kept open just for them and they were the only ones who didn't know why. The soldiers and other medical personnel circled them like a live studio audience.

"All right, then," Sanjay said. "If I were in your shoes, I suppose I'd want to know what I was cooperating with and why."

Rick, the primary subject of the doctor's interest, shifted in his seat.

"Without going into a lot of boring detail, we think the drug you've been taking, BioFuse, has potential to reverse what's happening outside."

"What *is* happening outside?"

"It's technical."

"It's not technical at all," Rick said. "A bunch of dead people got up and started walking. Then they started biting other people, and those people started walking, just like—"

"Like zombies, am I correct?" Sanjay was still smiling. "Yes. We have also reached that conclusion.

In truth, I can't answer your question. We don't know what's going on or why. What we do know is that some … *parameters* we've been watching spiked severely when it all began."

"What kind of parameters?"

"Tell me, Mr. Shelton, have you noticed any side effects while you've been on BioFuse?"

"What kind of side effects?"

"Oh, the usual. Dry mouth. Headache. Loss of appetite."

"No."

"Bizarre ideation. Unusual mental phenomena."

"Like ESP?"

Sanjay pulled out a tablet. "We intended BioFuse to help the brains of patients suffering with debilitative memory and cognitive impairments build new nerve cells. You see, when a person has, for instance—" he extended a hand toward Rick, "—Alzheimer's Disease, these tiny little buildups happen in the brain and slow it down."

"Plaques," Rick said. "I know this part. Move on."

"We thought we knew how the drug would work in patient brains, but it turns out we were wrong.

Or at least weren't always right. The agent at work in BioFuse sort of has a mind of its own."

"In what way?"

"It's not important." Sanjay waved a hand dismissively. "But because it's meant to 'work around the damage' instead of 'remove the damage,' it means your own body is an active participant. There's a lot of variability in that way, simply because every body and every person — and hence every response — is different. Much more than expected."

"Are you getting this?" Rick asked Thom.

Sanjay waved his hand again. "All right. Brass tacks. Here's what matters. You, Mr. Shelton, have an extremely resistant brain. I could show you. It's really quite fascinating in your scans."

Rick turned and looked meaningfully at Thom: *I told you they did scans.*

"You mean I'm strong," Rick said. "Mentally."

"I think he means 'stubborn,'" Carly said.

Sanjay pointed at her. "Precisely. I would like very much to be more scientific about this, but our working theory is far simpler than that. We believe your development path is unique because you have rigidly self-proscribed 'acceptable' ways that BioFuse is permitted, by your own rules, to build new connections. In a more malleable person, the new connections would be more straightforward because they themselves — and by that, I mean their brains and their bodies — are more straightforward."

"And?" Rick said.

"Again, it's complicated, but I think the unique function of your brain, combined with BioFuse, might actually be making you immune to certain … things."

"What makes you think that?"

Sanjay stumbled, a bit flustered. He seemed not to expect Rick's suite of questions, and Thom got the definite feeling he was having to improvise on a carefully written script.

"Certain boring medical metrics."

Thom looked at Carly for help. She was medical herself; she'd understand what the doctor wanted to say. But Carly's eyes were hard, pre-staring at him before he had a chance to stare at her. Very subtly, she shook her head: *No. Don't say what you're about to say.*

Thom returned to observing without a word.

"You think I'm immune," Rick said.

"Exactly."

"To a disease that *just* cropped up."

"Again I could bore you, but there are ways in which we anticipated … well, not *this* exactly, but a predilection for an anomaly in your case."

"And you think I'm immune despite the fact that I haven't been bitten. I haven't had a *chance* to be immune." He looked to Thom, Carly, and Brendan. "Why aren't you talking about *them* being immune? Or anyone else who hasn't been bitten?"

Thom shifted uncomfortably. Either Rick had forgotten Carly's bite or was deliberately obscuring it. She looked more waxen than ever. When would someone notice, and what would they do when they did?

"Give us some credit, Mr. Shelton. We have a lot of your medical history at our disposal, and of course I'm not exactly handing over all of our internal research. Suffice to say, you've been of interest to Hemisphere for a while."

"And that's why you've been doing extra tests on me."

"Correct."

Rick shook his head. He was mulling, trying to fit the pieces together. "This doesn't make any sense. You've been wondering about me for a while now, and now you think I might be immune … but it's all in the context of a disease that didn't exist this morning."

"It hadn't *manifested* this morning," Sanjay corrected.

"So, what, you knew it was coming or something?"

"No, no, of course not."

"What, then?"

Rick's no-bullshit voice was downright intimidating. In the silence after his question, they could all clearly hear the ticking of a wall clock.

"Think of it like this," Sanjay said, deepening Thom's sense that the man was improvising. "You're moving into a new house and you find a key. You don't know what that key's for, so you set it aside. Later, you find a chest in the attic with a padlock you can't open. Wouldn't it be logical to try the key you found months ago?"

Carly was still looking at Thom, her expression still begging his silence. Nothing Sanjay said made much sense. Thom had been assuming it was because it was over his head, but now he was starting to think it was because Sanjay wasn't actually saying much of anything at all.

The doctor must have sensed he was losing his

audience, so he stood and brushed his hands together. "Anyway. Shall we draw that blood?"

"Why did you take Rosie?" Rick asked. "She's not in your trial."

"Why did you take *any* of them?" Carly added.

Sanjay sighed and sat back down. "All right. I suppose with all these questions, I wouldn't feel like cooperating either." Another sigh. "What I am about to tell you is highly confidential, proprietary information, but we don't exactly have time to draft NDAs, so assuming there's another day for any of us, I'd appreciate if you could keep it to yourself."

"Seriously?" Rick asked.

"Not because it's illegal or immoral," Sanjay scrambled to add. "More because it would blow our methodology and, frankly, cost this company a lot of money and an equal number of valid test results. See, when you do a study of any sort, it's important that experimenters don't accidentally influence the outcome. We must administer whatever we're testing, BioFuse in this case, and then get out of the way. But because of the way BioFuse works and the varied nature of its results, a lot of what we do is to observe our subjects 'in the wild' as it were. We don't want to simply test you using our people and ask questions. It tells us much more when we can see how you act when you're not being observed. Or when you *think* you're not being observed."

"You spy on us?"

"That's putting it a little dramatically, but yes, in a limited way. Never in private, of course, but when you're out in public — say, at a mall — we want to see how you react. We want to see if BioFuse helps you navigate life in real-world situations."

"But Rosie ..."

Something hit the floor. All heads whipped around to see Carly, her eyes on the ground, embarrassed. She'd knocked her water over, and now it was everywhere.

"I'm sorry," she said.

"It's no problem." Sanjay went to the others, presumably to ask one to fetch a mop.

When the doctor wasn't looking, Carly moved close to Rick and whispered something.

Then she said, "You said there was somewhere to lie down? Where Rosie and the others are resting?"

"Oh! Yes, of course. The test will take a half hour or so anyway, and I believe we're quite safe here in the meantime." Sanjay motioned for one of the others to show Carly the way.

"No problem," said Rick, rolling up a sleeve. "Where do I go?"

Thom was confused. His father's questions were done, just like that?

Carly took Thom's hand and said, "Maybe you should come with me."

SIXTEEN

Kind of a Stretch

CARLY THANKED the woman who led them to the brightly lit back room, which turned out to be a short hallway leading to several more rooms. All but one, on cursory inspection, were empty. They found Rosie in the last one, on a cot flanked by many others, fast asleep.

"She's *sleeping?*" Thom asked.

Carly moved with purpose. She'd shut the door to the hallway after coming through and was now closing the door to their room, pulling a blind over the small window. She locked the door, thought, then unlocked it. "She's not sleeping. She's drugged."

"How do you know that?"

"Because Sanjay has a note about it on the lock screen of his phone."

"How do you know what he …" But she already had a device in her hand that didn't match any of his family's iPhones. "You stole his phone?"

"His lab coat was draped over the chair where I was sitting, and this was in the pocket."

"Carly, what's—?"

"Shh. Just listen." She shook her head. "He's lying. I don't know what parts exactly he's lying about, so I'm assuming all of it."

"How do you—?"

"I don't think he's a doctor. I mean, maybe like a PhD doctor, but not an MD. The stuff he was saying out there? None of it makes sense."

"What did you say to Rick out there?"

"I told him to let them draw his blood, but not to ask any more questions."

"Why not?"

"Because if Sanjay keeps talking, pretty soon he's going to trip over himself. And I'd rather he didn't. Right now, he probably assumes we believe him, but if Rick asks him something he can't answer, he'll know the jig is up."

She was handling the phone deftly, by the edges. She set it on a rolling tray, then rummaged in her purse. She'd probably have lost the thing by now, but it converted to a little backpack. All her stuff was still inside.

She pulled out a compact and a fat foundation brush, then swept it across the phone's surface.

"What are you doing?" Thom asked.

"The powder shows where the screen's been touched most often. See?"

He looked. After dusting, she'd woken the thing to reveal the code entry. The darkest smudges lined up with the 4, 6, 8, and 2 buttons.

"How do you know how to do that?"

"I thought you were cheating. Saw this little trick in *Cosmo* in an article on how to catch an unfaithful spouse."

"You thought I was ..." Thom couldn't believe it. He wished he had time or energy right now to feel betrayed.

"I know you're not. We can talk about it later." She was already tapping out all the combinations of those four digits, muttering thanks that Sanjay had stuck with a four-digit code rather than the more popular six. Knowing the digits, she needed only to find the order. Thom remembered this from high school math, concluding there were only twenty-four possible combos. Carly found it about halfway through.

In the interim, Thom was inspecting the room. Even less made sense now. Brendan said the Hemisphere people had rounded up a whole lot of people — five vans worth, he assumed. Sanjay had confirmed as much in the front room, but unless the building had hidden passageways, Rosie appeared to be the only one back here. The implications opened even more boxes. If they'd only taken Rosie, it seemed to suggest they'd only ever been looking for Rick. It was pretty much all Thom felt comfortable concluding.

"Okay," Carly said. "Most of what I was hoping to find is on a cloud server, and it looks like his local copies are encrypted. I found a bunch of promising email attachments, but they're all encrypted, too. But look at this. Sanjay must have sent this when he saw us outside or something. They've got an evacuation planned. The National Guard is coming to get them in less than an hour."

Thom looked through the windows. Evening was coming. "Good. What else?"

Carly looked frustrated. "There's probably a lot in here, but the only thing that's not encrypted are things like email and this messaging app they're using. I'd have to read everything he's got, and there's no time."

"What do you want to do?"

"I don't know that there's anything we can do. I'm telling you that what he said out there was bullshit, but I'm not sure it changes anything. The way he was tap-dancing, I get the feeling they've got a secret worth protecting. If we become a problem, they might not want us to leave. Or they might *force* us to leave — kick us out into the crowd, which is obviously getting larger by the bite."

Thom knew; he was still looking through the windows at the growing pile of gnashing humans outside the fence.

"Either way we're not getting out of the city without a ride," Carly finished. "I vote we cooperate like hell."

He went to Rosie and gently shook her. She began to stir, but it would take a while for her to fully wake.

Thom looked back at Carly. "Sanjay said they were watching their test subjects. Just observing them 'in the wild.'"

"Yeah. Wearing black suits with skinny black ties so they stand out? Armed with special weapons?

Five vans worth, and yet they sort through everyone and only take Rosie?"

"What, you think they wanted to lure Rick here, using her?"

"I think they wanted Rick, but he never came out."

"Why not wait longer? The place wasn't overrun yet."

"I don't know."

"Why not leave a note or something? How could they assume he'd know where to go?"

"I don't know."

"Why five vans?"

"Maybe they knew it would spread fast. Thought they'd need five vans to hold them all."

"But they didn't take the …" *Go on, say it.* "The zombies. They took Rosie instead."

"*I don't know,* Thom. I just know that what he told us out there was the biggest load of hand-waving bullshit I've ever heard. He was either making it up on the fly or he has no idea what he's doing. And did you see the other guy? The one in scrubs?"

"Yeah. I got the feeling he's the one calling the shots."

"The only thing I believe for sure is that they

want Rick. Sanjay asked about new mental capabilities, and we both know your father thinks he has some."

"You don't seriously think he's got some kind of ..." Jesus. This, he found harder to say than *zombies*. "Some kind of ESP connection to Rosie or something?"

"No idea." She was still scrolling through the phone. "I'm starting to get the feeling they think 'latent brain abilities' aren't consciously controlled. They're primal. *Sub*-conscious. Remember the time I *just knew* Brendan was in trouble, and you got so mad at me?"

Thom remembered just fine. They'd been planning a rare lunch over Brendan's summer vacation —just the two of them. He was almost thirteen and their neighborhood was a safe one, so they'd felt comfortable leaving him alone. But then Brendan decided to make afternoon toaster waffles and dropped a pad of butter, and he'd slipped on it, knocking himself out on the kitchen floor. They'd been about to sit when Carly insisted they go home; she was positive something was wrong.

Examples of maternal instinct were everywhere in the animal kingdom once you started to look for them.

Rick and Rosie had supposedly only met recently. But who knew? Rick kept his sensitive side under tight wraps, showing it only when forced. They might have been together for months. Even a year or more.

"I don't know, Carly. It's kind of a stretch."

"But does it matter? Here we are, right where they wanted us. Where they wanted *Rick*. Clearly he's special, just maybe not in the way they're pretending he is. My priority here is to get out first, not be played for fools a distant second." She shook her head, frustrated, and slipped Sanjay's phone back into her pocket. "But it looks like I may have to accept the second in order to accomplish the first."

Carly tried to stand, wincing on her bad ankle. Thom knelt before her, and glancing up for permission, raised her pants.

Her entire lower leg looked dead now. It was black, run through with even darker veins. He touched it and found he could feel her pulse. Low and slow, not like a trained athlete but like a body about to give up.

"I don't understand why this is moving so slowly." They had dubious opportunity to see more turnings, and almost all of the bitten turned bad before the Sheltons moved out of sight.

"Maybe it has something to do with Rick," Carly said.

"How? You're not related to Rick."

"No, but he likes me. Not in the way he likes Rosie, but …"

Thom understood. It'd been clear for a long time that Rick liked his daughter-in-law far better than his son. The idea that Rick was somehow tied to Rosie and Carly (and Brendan; he loved Brendan) was a long shot to be sure, but he was equally sure that if "psychic protection" applied here, he'd likely have none of it.

If Thom had been the one to get bitten instead of Carly, they might all be dead now.

Stupid idea. Stupid, baseless speculation.

"Maybe you should try and get some sleep," he said, seeing Carly flag.

But a terrible set of noises came before she could so much as lower her head.

SEVENTEEN

Mostly an Accident

RICK STILL DIDN'T LIKE needles, as much as he'd trained himself to endure in life.

He didn't avoid them the way some needle-phobes did, and he never availed himself of the considerations given to those who hated them. Watching TV, holding a loved one's hand, or anything like that. But he did always tune out the voice of whoever was drawing the blood when the time came, focusing all his energy on a lot of nothing at all. He didn't look at the needle or give a beat of his thought. The kiss of the tip was hard pressure, and not a thing more than that.

It was easier to stare at the corner and accept his impalement.

That's what Rick was doing when Sanjay slid

the needle into the pit of his arm. He felt the pressure, but then came a red-hot flare of pain.

He flinched. The still-unnamed woman in scrubs held his arm down at Sanjay's order, but Rick was already tensing and pulling away.

"Hold him!" Sanjay shouted, trying now to extract the needle.

Something had gone wrong. Blood was spritzing from the needle site, spraying the doctor's coat and face like a tiny little hose. When the needle finally came out, Rick's arm gushed in a river.

Sanjay aided his assistant's efforts to apply pressure, but it still took thirty seconds or more to stuff wadding over the draw site and wrap it clumsily with medical tape.

Rick's eyes went to the table, where Sanjay had set the syringe. There was blood inside it, but the needle had been bent almost thirty degrees at the tip. No wonder he was bleeding.

"You used a syringe?"

"Yes, yes," said Sanjay, trying to clean up.

"They usually use those vial things."

"Yes, well, I prefer a syringe."

But Rick's radar — maybe because he'd gained spooky intuition as a side effect of treatment, or maybe just because Carly's words had put him on alert — was already on high.

The syringe was out of the ordinary, and right now everything unusual was suspect. Syringes were for injecting, not typically drawing. But there was blood in it now, so of course Sanjay was telling the truth.

Except for that burn. He'd never had a blood draw burn like that before.

He looked at his arm while Sanjay removed and wiped his glasses, and the assistant went for a mop. It was bruising severely — all that blood now welling up under his skin. But even allowing for bruises, an odd color had stained one area on his ad-hoc bandage.

What could be staining it black?

"Did you inject me with something?"

"No. Of course not."

Rick grabbed for the syringe with his good hand.

Sanjay tried to stop him, but Rick Shelton could only be pushed so far. He was being manipulated and he knew it, and Sanjay, unless he was stupid, had to know that Rick knew it. What games were left to play?

He shoved the doctor's hand back, nearly

causing him to slip in the blood puddle on the floor.

On the vial was a handwritten label. It said, NECROSIS FACTOR.

"What did you put in me?"

"Nothing!"

"Don't lie!"

"Please. Keep your voice down." Sanjay's hands were up, making peace. "All right. Yes. Okay. But it's safe, I promise. We've all but concluded you're immune."

Rick stared at the syringe. They'd tried to fool him, and that really pissed him off. Injecting something and then using the same syringe to draw blood back out couldn't be clean protocol; it'd contaminate the sample. The fact that Sanjay had done it — and on the sly — meant one of two things. Either the draw wouldn't be ruined by trace amounts of the shit he'd been injected with, or the draw didn't matter.

Either way, Rick didn't like being a pawn.

"Did you ... Did you inject me with what *they* have?"

"Well, yes, but you'll be perfectly—"

"So you did do this!"

"No!" Sanjay shouted. "No, we extracted it from a corpse!"

"From a corpse?"

"Please, Mr. Shelton! Please calm down."

Rick was up in a second, taking Sanjay by the neck.

The assistant had returned to mop, so Rick jabbed a foot out to slam the door, locking all three of them inside. As Rick stood, he knocked the rolling tray to the floor, raising a clatter.

Sanjay was practically choking, shirt balled tight enough to smash his windpipe.

"You were at the mall for me," Rick said, his face inches from the doctor's.

"Sort of!"

"What the fuck's that mean?"

"You were *all* there! Everyone in your cohort!"

"My 'cohort'?"

"Your test group! Everyone who'd been given BioFuse! *Please*, Mr. Shelton!"

Rick relaxed his grip slightly, but moved so his back was to the door. The assistant looked mild enough, but he still kept watch on her hands, knowing the room was full of everyday objects ready to be used as weapons. And he did feel more or less safe, knowing that if they didn't need his voluntary cooperation, he'd either be dead of in handcuffs.

Help could be summoned by the pitch of their voices. There was more than enough firepower outside to neutralize one ex-Marine.

Rick was wondering if he should formally hold Sanjay hostage when there was a knock on the door.

"Doctor? Sir?"

It was one of the soldiers. The man in scrubs wouldn't sound so formal.

Rick glared, still holding tight. Sanjay said, "Yes?"

"Everything okay in there?"

"Oh yes. Yes, fine."

"Sounded like something fell over."

"I'm just clumsy, is all."

That made Rick relax more, as the footsteps walked away. He let the doctor go.

"What's going on here? For real this time."

"Okay," Sanjay said, and suddenly the most cordial parts of his personality were gone. He didn't become severe, but he did become serious. "The infection the public calls 'Rip Daddy' is mutating. We believe it's in a sort of 'adolescence' right now, halfway between a juvenile form and a more mature, evolved form of the same thing. Like any adolescence, it's a time of tumultuous change.

There is confusion and upheaval. Your grandson looks to be about that age. Perhaps you can relate."

Rick barely moved. He'd let go of Sanjay's neck, but he hadn't forgotten what they'd just done to him. He'd grown older, but he was sure he could still kill a person with his bare hands — and wanted both people in the room with him to understand that. Maybe they could call for help, but Rick bet he could take at least one of them down before the cavalry arrived.

"Eventually we believe the virus will stabilize, once it reaches a form that can find equilibrium with the rest of its ecosystem. For that to happen, though, requires a lot of experimentation on the virus's part. It needs to try this form and that form to see what works best. Those experiments could cost a lot of lives — but more importantly, by the time it *does* finally stabilize, it may well be beyond our ability to rein it in. That means we must battle it at the worst possible time, when the target is moving the fastest." He nodded toward Rick as if he were a prop. "And it means we must take some risks. Do some things we'd rather not, for the greater good."

"So you're trying to stop it."

"Of course we're trying to stop it. Halting the spread is Mr. Burgess's number one priority."

"How can it be his number one priority? It's brand new!"

Sanjay shook his head. "It's not new. It simply hit a critical developmental milestone. We've been tracking changes in wild type Rip Daddy for three months now."

"What does it have to do with me?"

Sanjay paused before answering. Another lie coming? Rick wasn't sure.

"BioFuse shows potential as a way to inoculate against mutated forms of Rip Daddy. Unfortunately, we think it's done just the opposite. Rather than protecting against the disease, one or more members of your cohort contracted a Rip Daddy strain that used BioFuse as a selection pressure."

"English, dammit," Rick said.

"It's like if you're attacked with a knife. Maybe you almost die, but if you don't die, now you know how to defend against a knife. We didn't go out there and infect the others in your trial; the goal was to develop immunity without introduction of the disease agent. But we think some of them contracted it anyway, and BioFuse did its best, but the result was like you winning that knife fight. It adapted. It 'learned how to defend against the knife,' which in this case was BioFuse. The result was stronger and more virulent than we ever could have suspected."

Rick didn't think Sanjay was telling him the whole truth. For instance: If someone caught Rip Daddy while on BioFuse, how was it spreading so fast — and why did it start (at least partially) at the mall? They saw at least three of these things there. Unless all three, quite independently, were bitten by a single creature before coming in?

"Why did you have five vans at the mall?"

"Because as I said, your entire test group was at the mall."

"How did you manage that?"

"Subtle psychological manipulation. It's complicated."

"There were supposed to only be two subjects per county."

"That wasn't technically true."

"What about Miles Pope?"

"You know Miles Pope?"

"I know him enough." Rick shoved the doctor to remind him that this wasn't just a conversation; he was still the one with a metaphorical knife to their throats. "He keeps popping into my mind."

"He does? Would you say it feels … extrasensory?"

"Never mind your bullshit! What's Pope to you?"

"Well, he's not insignificant, and that makes your question just now noteworthy indeed. Our best guess pegs Pope as the one who first contracted Rip Daddy. The one in whom the new illness first manifested."

It was a diversion. "What were you planning to do at the mall? Why did you make sure we were all there at the same time?"

"Well …"

Rick moved closer. His hand rose as if to, again, grab the man's throat.

"All right," he said. "We felt it was necessary to see what would happen. That required a large population sample, in an enclosed space, to test varied forms of the virus."

"In what way?"

"Miles Pope's form is nearly stable. It develops slowly, without the frenetic burn-out of most of what you've seen today. Our hope was that a random toss in a contained population, some of whom were on BioFuse, like you, and some of whom were not …"

Now Rick really did grab him again. "Holy shit. You *let* that outbreak happen."

"In a controlled fashion!" Sanjay blurted. "Some of the variants are incredibly aggressive, so a fixed, closely observed study in a wild setting—"

"With real people? Real human beings?"

"Acceptable losses! Rip Daddy is already out there, and it's nationwide. The question of its evolving into a deadly form was a question of *if*, not *when*. We had two choices: either conduct a single, closed-system experiment under the supervision of our people, that we could control, utilizing a potential inoculant we felt had enormous potential to stabilize and eventually eliminate the mutant forms … or we could let the same thing happen at a random time, in a random place, where we couldn't control it or slow the spread at all!"

"And how's that working for you? The whole fucking city is infected!"

"Yes! It is! But we are not careless, Mr. Shelton. We always planned contingencies atop contingencies."

Rick felt cold. His fist slackened involuntarily. "That's why the military was already here. Because you figured if you couldn't contain it at the mall, you could at least contain the city."

"It was the best we could do. It's densely populated, under half a million to limit exposure, but still large enough to provide a statistically significant test."

Rick tossed the doctor back again, then looked at his bruised arm. "So? Am I immune?"

"You received an intravenous dose of the most virulent strain we know so far. If you weren't immune, you'd be changed by now. Not that you were the only one taking the risk. You do understand, the two of us voluntarily got in this room with you. We could have contained you for it. Given it to you through bars in a cage."

"You're champs. Thanks."

"Mr. Shelton, please, try to understand. I don't blame you for resenting our methods, but I promise, this was the only way. We need you."

"That's why you took Rosie, and let the others go."

"We saw you with her. We wanted to study your connection and that could only be done here. But you were never in any danger, and we'd have brought you here if you hadn't 'tuned in' and come on your own to get her. We've never taken eyes off you, Mr. Shelton. You may not always have seen us, but we've been right behind you all day." Sanjay held up both hands, trying to make peace. "Your immunity, whether it's due to a 'stubborn' brain or something else we've yet to determine, might be what BioFuse wasn't. It's better this way, so long as you agree to serve your fellow man. The drug was developed to treat Alzheimer's. It was always a stop-gap. Discovery of its affinity for Rip Daddy was mostly an accident."

"Mostly?"

Sanjay continued. "But you? You developed immunity in the wild, or always had it. With your cooperation, we might be able to prevent this from happening again in other cities. We might be able to make a vaccine, or find ways to stimulate brains to be more resistant, like yours."

Rick had heard enough. The little shit was defending mass murder. Hitler had claimed aspirations for the greater good in exactly the same way.

"That's a pretty good story." Then in one quick motion, Rick grabbed the doctor, spun him around, grabbed a scalpel from the shelf, and pressed it against the man's throat. "But instead, how about I use you as a human shield to get out of here?"

"Please! There are seventeen armed soldiers outside this door!"

"I guess you'd better convince them, then."

Rick's non-scalpel hand relaxed, prepping to reach for the knob.

"WAIT!"

Rick didn't want to hear another word, but something in the doctor's tone made him stop.

"What?"

"Your daughter-in-law. She's bitten."

"And?"

"The fact that she's still coherent means she must have contracted the Pope strain. Whatever attacked her had probably been changing over the course of weeks, then self-realized when all the others reached critical and started to—"

"Make sense, dammit."

"There's a treatment!" Sanjay spat, stuttering against the blade on his throat. "It's still experimental, but it's been effective in mice. It's the only chance she's got — otherwise she'll turn just like the rest of them!"

Rick let go, but he didn't drop the scalpel. Sanjay, knowing he'd scored a hit, adjusted his collar.

"Help us and don't reveal what we've discussed here, Mr. Shelton," he said, now less panicked. "Do that, and we can keep your daughter-in-law alive."

EIGHTEEN

What Bakersfield?

Thom could tell something terrible had almost gone wrong, or had already but nobody was talking about it.

The way Rick emerged with Sanjay and the tech (both sweating, Sanjay disheveled) was full of unfriendly body language and unspoken truths. Thom tried to ask; Rick brushed him off like swatting a fly. He was handling things his own way no matter what anyone else thought or cared, same as he always had.

Rick had a huge bruise on his arm, wrapped in gauze. Despite the shouting and crashing, Rick said it was an accident, like the arm, and that everyone could just trust him and let it go. Thom thought of reminding him that he was an Alzheimer's patient and that Thom was technically still his guardian, but doing so felt like a phenomenally bad move.

He wasn't feeble at all right now, and truthfully hadn't been for weeks, maybe months. He insisted that his brain scans revealed something in the neighborhood of a cure, not remission, and while Thom had doubted it at first, he certainly wasn't about to doubt it now. Once your father was right about zombies, pretty much everything else was off the table.

There were more medical tests and proddings with needles, but this time Rick did them in the middle of the main room, almost defiantly. A new stern expression — one he hadn't worn when Thom and Carly had gone for the nap that'd never happened — dominated his features. Rick was a strongman all over again, but instead of making him feel confident, it made Thom feel weak. His father had always been a man's man. By implication, he'd always been something less.

They waited. Brendan found a stack of games from when the place had been a clinic, stored in a wall cupboard. They were a bit young for him, but Thom, Brendan, an increasingly sick Carly, and even Rosie played anyway. The game was called *Uncle Wiggly* — familiar only to Rosie, from her childhood. Though she'd been spacey all day, she was rock solid at the board game. Brendan complained, with surprisingly good humor, that Rosie was making up the rules.

When the last game they could stand ended, Brendan's face fell like a pile of bricks. He'd glanced at his mother, who hadn't simply exhaled and said, "That was fun" like normal, but had instead fallen back against the waiting room couch like a person relieved of strenuous duty. This seemed to remind him of something he'd been trying not to think about, before sending him to read old magazines alone in the corner.

Rick came over. It was late by now and the day had been impossibly long. Even he was sagging.

He sat beside his son.

Thom looked over as if the old man had made a mistake and not yet realized.

Rick handed him a syringe. "It's not the zombie thing that's making her sick. It's sepsis."

"What?"

"Bacterial infection in her blood. From the biter's plain old human saliva."

Rick looked down at the syringe. "What's this?"

"Antibiotics. I suggest having Carly try giving it to herself if her hands are steady."

"You don't think I can do it?"

"I think you're untrained, like me. She's done this before."

"Not on herself."

"What?" Rick started to stand, then slapped Thom on the back. "You guys never do heroin?"

His father turned with an unlikely smile on his face. He looked so tired.

"Dad."

"Yeah."

"What happened while Carly and I were in the back?"

"Nothing."

The shortness of his father's response made him angry. "You think I can't handle it?"

"I think you can handle it just fine. This is just the way it has to be."

"Why are you keeping secrets?"

"Because I have to." It sounded like such a strangely proper answer.

"*Dad,*" he said when Rick turned again.

"Yeah," his father answered, looking down.

"How do you know it's not the disease?" Quieter: "Carly, I mean."

"It's too fast," Rick answered.

"But they turn fast."

"Not Carly."

"Why?"

"Just trust me, Thom."

"DAD."

Rick turned a third time. He should be exasperated, but he seemed exhausted more than anything else.

"I'm sorry I didn't believe you."

"I wouldn't have believed me either. I'm sorry I was right."

Do it. Take the risk. So Thom said, "You haven't ever really believed in me, have you?"

A baiting question. He was sure Rick would deny it, but instead he said, "What have you given me to believe in, Thom?"

"I have a good job. A good wife. A good life."

"Those are things that happened to you."

"I had to *get* the job. I had to *get* the wife."

"Either that or they got you. I had to *get* Alzheimer's."

"God damn you."

Rick surprised him again, this time with a nod. "That's fair."

"Why are you like this?"

Rick came closer. "It's not that I don't love you, Thomas. You're my son. I have to love you, just like you have to love me. But even beyond that, I always did my best."

"You did shit."

"You're right. I did. I picked a side, and that side made me an asshole. What's always bothered me about you is that you couldn't even do that. You've always gone down the middle. You took the job that came to you. You took the woman who had to chase you down and make something happen, and you got damn lucky it was Carly who found you. You bought your own house straight out of my house, and you did it with your mother's insurance money. You've never had to make monthly rent, or a mortgage. You've never fought for a promotion or for your country."

"Not everyone has to—"

"I know. Not everyone has to. But you have to do *something*, Thom. *Anything*. You can't walk right down life's middle and see what comes. You can't join the Cub Scout troop just because your mom decides she wants to be a den mother. You can't take all the default classes in high school and college. I only ever had one complaint with you, and at first it really was just *one*. When you were ten, I wanted you to put yourself out there *once*. Take *one* big risk. But look what happened? You ignored me and ignored me and ignored me, until you finally decided I was the boogeyman. After that it was a mix of spite and digging in your heels. You were so determined to not be like me that passive acceptance became your entire life. Now it's who you are, and I see no sign that you're going to change."

"Why the hell should I change for you?"

Rick sighed, and for a minute Thom thought he might sit. "That's what you keep refusing to understand. You shouldn't do it for me. We had our chance. You should do it for your son."

"Brendan is just fine." Thom wasn't as angry as he wanted to be. Maybe he was tired too, but there was a much worse reason waiting in the shadows. It was possible, finally, that he was seeing *all* of his father's points, not just the ones having to do with paranoia and the end of the world.

Maybe he agreed with what Rick was saying.

Maybe the past day of inaction and evasiveness had proven it to be true.

"He's just fine," Rick agreed. "In fact, he's better than fine. He's bold; he's got real opinions; he protects his family and seems bent on doing the right thing. But that's despite you, not because of you. I already see him starting to retreat. From you, sure, but also from himself. Soon you'll have trained that spirit right out of him. Soon he'll only be good at playing it safe."

"Safe is the reason we're still breathing, Dad," Thom said.

A long moment before his only reply. "Is it?"

Time passed.

It seemed to take too long.

Even as Brendan and Carly fell asleep (she was looking better already, though her wound was still a sewer), Thom found himself willing but unable to do the same. His nerves stayed too high, and that made him ponder his father's words. When he'd been forced into fights, he'd gotten through them and felt calmer. By contrast, turning a blind eye only made the tension endure, and grow over time.

"How much longer?" Thom asked Sanjay.

"It's not the tests holding us up. It's the Army," he answered.

"What about them?"

"I think they're worried about extracting us too early."

"Why?"

"Because they aren't finished setting up. You and us, we've got a deal. I said I'd get you out and I keep my promises. The five of you will have to quarantine for days or maybe even months to be sure you haven't brought anything out with you, probably at our new Aberdeen Valley facility, but you will leave Bakersfield. Just be patient. If we leave too soon, people afterward will start to ask why others didn't get to go. We need to get out at the very last minute, for reasons of public perception."

Afterward. Too soon. Very last minute. Thom didn't like the implication.

"What are they going to do with Bakersfield?"

"What Bakersfield?" Sanjay answered.

Another half hour.

Another hour.

Still Thom couldn't sleep, now that his conscience was so heavy.

Even if his family got out, he doubted he'd ever shake the survivor's guilt — passive and at the mercy of an external force again, just like his father said.

Past midnight, Sanjay entered. Thom was already awake, and he shook the others. Rick, beside Rosie, roused on his own.

"They're predicting another half hour," he said.

"Did they call you?" A leading question; Thom wanted to know if Sanjay had noticed his missing phone.

He shook his head. “They called my boss.”

“I thought you were the boss.”

“It’s sort of a matter of perception.”

“What about the tests?” Rick asked.

“We have all we need, I think. I’m sure we’ll call on you again while you’re quarantined, but my guess is you’ll be so thoroughly bored, you’ll leap at the chance for something to do. I don’t have any results to share. To be honest, what we’re seeing is … unhelpful.”

“How?”

“You are unique to you, Mr. Shelton. We seem to have called you here only to find out that what keeps the virus from attacking you cannot be replicated. But look on the bright side: if you hadn’t come, you wouldn’t be about to leave.”

Fifteen more minutes.

The building was lit, but without any sun the gloom draped their lives like a blanket. Thom was beyond exhausted. Carly, Brendan, and Rick all looked about the same. Only Rosie appeared chipper when she woke.

Maybe he could close his eyes … rest for a few minutes.

Thom was just starting to nod off when—

NINETEEN

Don't Look

THE FRONT DOOR EXPLODED OPEN.

It sounded like a bomb had gone off, but it was actually a car driving through the door and most of the wall, causing the front roofline to collapse.

Bricks and dust rained from the broken ceiling. The whole room shook.

Thom pulled Brendan back and Carly, still clammy but now faster on her feet, leapt with them.

Rick stood almost calmly, but then even more chaos began.

Two people spilled out of the car, a man and a woman. The impact had broken their windshield and bent their doors, so they climbed across the hood. The hole was wide. Behind it, Thom could see a similar hole in the gate. One of the big Army trucks had moved, probably to make way for the coming evac, and apparently these joyriders had been waiting for a way inside.

But in saving themselves, they'd doomed those already in the building. The moonlight showed them plenty; Thom could see how fast the dead outside had multiplied … and how steadily, now that the perimeter was breached, they were ambling toward the bright light — and fresh meat — inside.

Two of the soldiers had been knocked either dead or unconscious by overhead debris, but the other dozen-plus sprang into action, dashing past the newcomers and their car to face the oncoming horde.

Thom could already hear similar gunfire (some of it louder and deeper, as if from a turret gun) from the building's sides, suggesting that all those vehicles forming the barricade weren't just for show. There were soldiers in them — more than thirty, probably, holding the building, along with all their vehicles and weapons.

He had a moment to consider it in one run-on thought *(this place must be serious even the military knows it's serious)* but after a second of that he was being pulled back by his father, who'd picked up one of the fallen soldier's guns.

He looked at Thom, who reservedly picked up the second dropped weapon.

Rick fired.

Soldiers outside did the same.

But Thom didn't fire; he either wasn't loaded or couldn't find a safety.

He wrestled the big gun for five seconds or so before the soldiers outside began to back into the car hole, removing any chance of a clean shot. At first Thom felt protected. Between him and the zombies was a line of trained and armed killers. But the line did not hold. There were too many creatures outside, and machine guns, as it turned out, ran dry much faster than movies had Thom imagining.

They fired in short bursts, but the total firing time seemed only seconds long — no more than ten. They must have had new magazines, and when they ran dry, Thom saw the soldiers reach to their belts.

But the hesitation was too long, and the walkers behind weren't frightened back when those in front of them were shot. Many, Thom noticed, weren't even hit right. Many of the soldiers weren't aiming for heads, or otherwise missing them entirely.

In fear, they seemed to be reverting to their training: hit that big target on the chest. Some of the walkers who made it inside had been shot so many times, Thom could practically see the outside-mounted lights through their bodies. And yet still they marched on.

Less than a minute after the car breached the wall, the walkers were inside and most of the soldiers were on the ground with walkers atop them, ripping away every bit of flesh they could reach.

Thom could hear the soldiers screaming.

Until they suddenly stopped after fifteen seconds, or fewer.

"Get in back!" Thom shouted, waving at Brendan, Carly, and Rosie.

Rick, still beside him, looked over surprised.

What, he didn't even think his son could yell?

Brendan came forward, double-clutching while trying to reach for a weapon.

Rick didn't see; he was doing something to Thom's gun, presumably to make it fire.

Thom saw just fine. The first soldier reached

back, taking him by the wrist with a reanimated hand.

Rick got the alert, but in helping Thom, he'd manage to tangle his gun's strap. He yelled, but then the thing's head exploded before he could so much as stand upright.

At first Thom didn't know what had happened, but then he felt heat on his left hand where it held the barrel, and saw that the muzzle was smoking.

He'd done it, and not by accident.

He'd had to raise the muzzle, aim, and fire.

The creature didn't even flinch a second time. Its brain was gone.

Rick looked at him as the memory eked back, Thom now recalling the instinct that made him take aim. There wasn't time for it — the first line of walkers was still trying to get around the car and over the bodies, but an enormous group was right behind them. It seemed like the city was already lost, half the citizens right outside as if called to a beacon.

Thom looked back. Carly was finally at a loss and Rosie seemed utterly confused.

"Brendan!" He hissed at his son.

"I want to help, Dad!"

"Get in back with your mother!"

Rick said, "He wants to help, Thom."

But Thom wasn't backing down this time. Righteousness was on his side; he knew it as surely as he knew how he'd made his first kill. He knew why he was right (and Rick was wrong) only after looking back again at Carly and Rosie. His wife was up to this but also injured, and that made them both fresh meat.

"He needs to do what's best, Dad," Thom told Rick.

"So why don't you cut the apron strings and—"

"And what's *best* is to protect them, not us."

Rick looked back and must have understood because his next noise was a bark of agreement at the boy. Carly's shock was here at last. If someone didn't force them into the rear, they weren't going to go.

And then it would all be over.

"GO!" Thom shouted.

Brendan was so startled by such an order coming from his father that he snapped-to without blinking.

Thom, armed now with his safety off, fired on repeat, scoring more hits than he'd have thought possible. But the line was several levels deep; they came like eager crowds at a lightning sale. He kept his burst short, just like the soldiers' and Rick's, but still he ran out quickly.

Rick thrust another magazine into his hands. They both reloaded. Thom was surprised to find the process fast, easy, and intuitive.

"Now you, Thom," Rick said.

"I'm fine where I am." And he *was* fine where he was, right beside the remaining soldiers.

Rick shoved him. "I'm not being noble. Nothing out here survives. I'll be right behind you."

Thom looked around. The soldiers were retreating — not away from the battle at large, but strategically, toward the door through which Brendan had just gone.

"You first," Thom said.

"Don't be stupid. I'm a better shot."

So he went, keeping his gun out, paranoid the entire time that his nerves would make him hit the trigger and kill the wrong target. Once Rick eclipsed him, he let the weapon hang on its strap.

Rick, last through, closed the door.

They were in that sparsely lit back hallway now, packed to the gills. Thom saw Sanjay and the female tech who'd helped with Rick's tests, but there was no sign of the other man, meaning

Sanjay was in charge for real now if he hadn't been before.

Three of the soldiers had made it, and the clamor behind the door and through the outside walls suggested there'd be no more. Anyone still in the lobby or outside the building could count their remaining life in minutes.

Carly was on a bench along the hallway's wall, sitting with one arm around a terrified-looking Rosie, and the other wrapped around her son.

"That's everyone," said Rick, taking charge.

"Hardly everyone!" Sanjay cried out.

"Everyone who matters," Rick replied. "Anyone hurt? I mean, more than usual?"

Too late, Thom realized that the soldier beside him was breathing far too heavy, and had been since they'd all fallen into place. He turned to look and saw the final seconds of humanity drain from the man's yellowing eyes.

Arms came up, one with a huge bite from the meat of his forearm. It looked like a Fourth of July watermelon — one chomped by an enthusiastic cartoon character. But the hands were strong; Thom felt fingers curve to compress his esophagus, tension in those macerated limbs pulling Thom into the soldier's maw.

A blow came from nowhere.

It wasn't Rick; he was at the group's front, seeing this but too distant to react with a clear line of sight. It wasn't Carly; she still looked dazed. With shock Thom found himself gazing into his son's furious face. He held a hammer, from a toolbox found in the hall. The claw end of the same hammer was embedded in the former soldier's skull — right at the back where the fissures met.

Brendan let go of the handle and the hammer fell with the body. It was like the axe from earlier. Only this one in miniature, swung by a smaller set of arms but no less effective.

"Are … Are you okay, Dad?" Brendan asked.

Thom swept his son into a bone-crushing hug.

"I'm sorry. I had to do something. I couldn't just—"

Thom held him by both shoulders and said, "I don't ever want you to be sorry again."

A window broke in one of the rooms at the hallway's end. Then another and another. On the opposite side, the locked door bulged, retracted, bulged again. They were either slamming against it to open the thing or simply applying the combined pressure of a hundred stacked bodies. Either way,

Thom could hear the members strain: hinges soon to give, a lock soon to snap.

The others — the ones who'd broken windows — appeared at the hall's end. It was maybe thirty feet, no more. Unlike on the opposite side, there was no door to stop them. There was also nowhere to go. They couldn't go back the way they'd come, and one peek into the other rooms showed their windows covered with shadows marching by outside.

Maybe the things were too dumb to know they could come in that way (the windows they'd broken were in a brightly lit room), but there'd be no getting past them if Thom and company cared to chance that way out. He could see the building as if from the air, inside his mind. They'd surrounded the building and were now pressing in. No escape whatsoever.

Brendan hugged his father. Carly and Rosie, strangers before today, huddled close. Thom saw Rick close his eyes; he suspected Rick's gun was empty and knew his goose was cooked. The others had wide eyes, waiting. One soldier still had ammo, so he fired and felled two of those coming. But then he ran dry too, and kept pulling the trigger until his pistol was empty. Thom did the same with his reloaded weapon … and then it was *really* over, with death now on everyone's doorstep.

"Don't look," Thom said, holding his son's shoulders. "Never look up."

A second crash shook the building. Dust rained from the ceiling, and elsewhere they could hear the sounds of falling metal, plaster, and glass. A cloud had bloomed ahead, thick enough that they could no longer see the zombies. When it cleared, Thom saw the nose end of an armored Jeep where the walkers had been, smashed through the end-of-hallway window and the small plaster wall beneath it.

"DOWN! GET DOWN!"

Thom did as he was told, and not a moment too soon.

The second the remaining living in the hallway hit the deck, the turret gun began to fire like the drag of a chain across a steel edge — far too fast to hear individual reports. But soon the walkers had been reduced to many piles of undead flesh.

The gunner waved them forward, shouting. *"Let's go, let's go!* This is evac! We leave in ten!"

He meant seconds. Thom was barely aboard when the Jeep started backing out, the gun silent but the gunner swinging the thing around on its mount.

There were another two Jeeps beyond the wall, each with a center-mounted minigun cutting semi-circles from the mass of oncoming walkers. There were so many of them. Thousands, Thom thought.

Had it really been this morning that things had been so normal?

An officer rushed to Sanjay, covered by gunfire. They spoke, then broke apart.

The crew was so much smaller than they'd been anticipating carrying out of the city.

"Hold tight and stay low." The driver swung his head toward the gunner while shifting the transmission into drive. "You know. Unless you want a haircut."

One of the new arrivals moved to the compromised barricade, just inside the circle and waving the Jeeps through. He pointed to one without any occupants other than a driver and gunner, then the other, lining them up as One and Two. Those Jeeps were supposed to be full of soldiers and staff, Thom assumed, but all those zombies had changed that. Now they were in the lead, meant to slice through the horde so the sole occupied Jeep could come from the rear.

With the miniguns cutting a swath through the crowd and the Jeeps behind, Thom found himself wondering how they were driving so smoothly. Shouldn't they be running over bodies?

Then he saw that all three vehicles had been fitted with old-fashioned cow-catchers like they used to put on the front of trains.

The bodies rolled aside.

The Jeeps rolled on.

TWENTY

No Longer Fit to Pull the Trigger

THE CROWDS OPENED up once away from Hemisphere.

Bakersfield's residents had the full city to spread out in, so the hordes couldn't be this dense everywhere. Wreckage was the biggest problem, but the Army guys had thought of that, too. Metal logjams were rammed at just the right angle and with just the right speed to shove them away from the cow catchers, same as the bodies.

Rick seemed uneasy.

Thom repressed an instinctual urge to avoid his father and moved closer. "What's bugging you?"

"Other than the zombies? Honestly, it's our company."

Thom looked ahead. They'd stopped once the

roads cleared, to distribute passengers evenly between the Jeeps. Two of their remaining soldier-guards were in the front Jeep with new guns in their hands, Sanjay and his tech were in the second, and the entire Shelton clan was in the rear Jeep, like a caboose in the back. They were more crowded than the others, but Thom would damn anyone who so much as *tried* to split them up now.

"You mean Sanjay?"

"I mean all of them. Sanjay told me some things I don't think he wants anyone else to know."

"But he needs you. You're helping."

"Yes. For now he needs me. He says the whole world might need me."

"He said inside that you're a dead end."

Rick nodded. "Maybe. But I also know they haven't played straight from the beginning. My guess is there's still a chance, but then what? We're a liability."

"Officially, only you know," Thom said.

"Officially. But they must know I'll tell you guys eventually."

"What are you saying?"

Rick didn't have to respond. Sanjay answered for him almost as if the man had been listening. They were nearing the city's edge; Thom could tell by a swarm of helicopters above the border in a semicircle. With little left to go, Sanjay said something to his driver, who picked up the radio and called the Sheltons' driver, and then the man started reaching for his holster. Their saviors must not have known whether Sanjay was done with Rick yet, so they'd taken everyone. Now that the pieces were settling back into place and their shared secrets were soon to come out, Sanjay had decided it was best to sweep the floor.

Rick understood. He leapt on the driver, pinning his gun hand to his side.

The Jeep, suddenly without hands on the wheel, skidded and nearly tipped.

It hit the side wall of a bistro, smashing glass, raining it into all their hair.

Rick got the man around his neck while the other Jeeps went on ahead, but the soldier was too strong and Rick just a little too far past his prime. He had him pinned, but the soldier immediately started prying him off.

Rick compensated with bodyweight; he wedged next to the driver and let gravity squeeze them into a single seat. Unbalanced, the driver reached for the stopped vehicle's sides, but Rick must have gotten his foot to the gas because he reached for the shifter, put the Jeep in reverse, and floored it in a rubber-squealing backward arc.

"HIT HIM!" Rick bellowed.

Thom was too far, but Brendan leapt the seat like a hurdle to comply.

He put a size-ten Converse in the man's face, striking hard enough to rattle some teeth. He lost his grip on wheel and sides. Combined with another touch of the accelerator, the driver tumbled over the half-door to the ground.

At the same time, Carly leapt onto the gunner's back. He hadn't seen it coming, especially from the rear. She somehow got him into a full nelson and, surprising everyone, it was Rosie who punched him — not in the gut as Carly probably intended, but in the balls.

He squealed, buckled, fell. Thom gave the final shove and Rick hit the gas.

Ten seconds later they were back on track … but marked for death by the border guards without question.

Rick hauled ass after the other Jeeps, but they were almost to a checkpoint ahead.

"We'll never get through," Thom said.

"Oh yes, we will."

Carly fished a phone from her pocket. Only, it wasn't hers. It was Sanjay's.

Thom watched her text whoever he had messaged about evacuation before. She wrote, *FIRST TWO JEEPS COMPROMISED. THIRD JEEP CLEAN.*

"They … They'd *know*, though, right?" Thom said. "They'd know who's up front and who's in the rear?"

A fireball bloomed. The first Jeep rolled sideways, and then its gas tank exploded. For the second shot, Thom had found the source and trained his eyes. This time he saw the RPG launched. It struck the second Jeep right in the center — no rolling away for that one.

Rick floored it. But in the dark of midnight, the fireball from all that detonated gasoline burned like a second sun, and in its glow Thom could see walls of zombies closing in from both sides.

It was a much larger group than before.

The gap to the gate closed. A simple cow catcher wouldn't be enough to plow through this furiously swarming horde.

"Shit," said Rick.

Carly pointed. "Look. Maybe we can get by over there."

Thom turned his head. He saw what she meant, but there was still no way. The rightmost group of oncoming dead had a long tail behind it, all walking toward the flames like moths to a lantern, but they weren't moving quickly. Their group was a bunch of sitting ducks, waiting for the zombies to cross like sacred cows across an Indian street.

And in the meantime, there was commotion from the ad-hoc tower from which the RPGs had been launched. It was difficult to see from this distance, but Thom was willing to bet he knew what was happening. Carly had confused them with her message from Sanjay's phone, but they weren't entirely stupid. They'd soon figure out what had gone down, and it looked to Thom like they were reloading the launcher.

They had two choices: Stay where they were and be blown up, or charge for the gap right now … and get swallowed by walkers.

No way out.

Unless …

Thom stood. He'd been toeing an equipment locker at his feet, and inside he'd noticed a most unusual road kit: flares, a jack, and one of those blunderbuss weapons he'd seen Hemisphere agents carrying in the mall.

He picked it up, deciding it looked simple enough to use. There was a switch on the side: ON/OFF. That plus a conventional trigger seemed to tell the whole story.

"You can't shoot them all, Thom," Carly said.

"I don't need to shoot them all," he grimly replied.

He got out. Carly watched him, arms on Brendan as if to hold him back. She must be starting to understand. By the way she held their son, she must be starting to see.

He moved to the Jeep's front, just outside Rick's driver door. There was no window; the thing had an open top for shooting. Thom looked down at his father.

Rick said, "I can do it, son."

Thom shook his head. "You said it yourself: there might still be something in you that helps them."

Rick's face held a curious emotion. Stern, yes, but something else as well. Something Thom had never seen from his father before. Maybe two or three things.

"I don't want to help them."

"Then help *them*." Thom ticked his head toward Carly, Brendan ... and yes, even Rosie.

Behind Rick, Carly was shifting, truly understanding at last. He had to move quickly. He didn't have the strength for what she had in mind, and if Carly tried to play hero, this might all be for nothing.

"You're sure?" Rick asked.

Thom nodded. "I'm sure."

He took a slow breath, then grasped his son by the forearm. "I'm proud of you, Thomas."

Thom could only give a grim nod. He couldn't face his father's eyes and he certainly couldn't look more rearward, to where Carly and Brendan were both starting to speak. To resist.

Without the strength to look back, he ran.

He heard Carly and Brendan shout after him, but he didn't have time for that right now; no way and no how could he take *that* in this moment. It took everything he had to pump his legs. To aim for the burning Jeeps and the center of this melee.

Thom fired his weapon once he got close. He didn't know how far it would shoot, but he aimed at the stragglers anyway — the ones he had to hurry up. The gun gave a mighty whistle like launching a mortar shell, then two of the zombies at the back of the group broke in half, their heads popping like squished grapes.

Encouraged and shouting now, Thom kept running. This time he aimed at the clot's center, but the gun seemed to need a recharge between shots.

They came on while he waited, looking down as he ran, watching a small gauge turn from red to yellow to green. Once green, he fired again. He only got one this time, but he was near enough to his target that the thing simply blew like a bomb.

But it was working; between the sight of Thom running and the sound of Thom's shouts and, somehow, the fury of Thom's weapon, the dead were coming fast. Those at the rear, eager for a meal and afraid it'd be gone by the time they reached the front, accelerated their pace, same as the ones he had seen in the mall and the city.

Thom watched his father drive maniacally into the gap at the rear, throwing a few stragglers high and wide with the modified front end. The dead came, still fast, still clearing the way. Thom saw the Jeep through the gate and into a waiting crowd of onlookers and press, knowing they'd be safe now; the Army wouldn't jettison them in front of all those civilians.

He'd done it.

He'd been brave.

He'd made his stand.

Now, Thom had to find a way out.

He fired, blowing six or seven away in a semicircle.

But there were too many.

And by the time the gauge turned green again, his finger was no longer fit to pull the trigger.

TWENTY-ONE

Dead City

Carly insisted on civilian quarters. She wanted to trust the Army, but this close to Bakersfield, they were hopelessly entangled with Hemisphere. They ended up in low-income housing. The neighborhood hadn't been especially good before, but now — thanks to the comparative despair of Bakersfield — it seemed just fine.

It'd been fifteen days, and Carly was all cried out. Brendan too, though he was fourteen and only had so many tears to publicly shed. He stuck to his room a lot more than he had before, and Carly knew it'd just take time.

Only two weeks, and they were both walking an incongruous balance. Thom was gone, but he'd died to save them. That, at least, meant something.

In time they could be proud, once the hurt was gone.

There was a knock on the door. For some reason Carly expected Rick, but of course he and Rosie had rented an RV in the Nevada desert just five days after the borders closed. He had a hunch that things would get worse before they got better — and as with all things Rick lately, that was already proving true.

Carly had stopped seeing him as off his rocker and started seeing him as something like an oracle. They talked on the phone daily, and then she always handed it over to Brendan … and neither he nor Rick ever divulged the nature of their discussions. She had a good guess anyway.

"Hello," said the newcomer. He was moderate height with black hair, small round glasses, and a neat little goatee. He had handsome, birdlike features. "My name is August Maughan."

Carly blinked. "You are, aren't you?"

He smiled. "Does my reputation precede me?"

"Almost as much as Archibald Burgess's. But … I thought you left Hemisphere?"

"I did. May I come in?"

Gobsmacked, Carly let him in, closed the door, and entered her shabby living room to find he'd already taken himself a seat on the couch. She sat in her usual chair opposite him.

"To answer your question, Archibald — Mr. Burgess — doesn't know I'm here. I'm afraid he's been a bit of a prickly pear on the matter."

"Why are you here?"

"Permission to resume? I'm afraid I don't have much time. I know Colonel Calais, who's in charge of this sector, and he sort of … owes me a favor. He said I could have ten minutes before my gate card no longer works. So unless you'd like me to move in with you—"

Carly smiled. The man was as charming in person as he'd been on TV, back when he and Burgess were partners. "Sorry. It's a two-bedroom."

"—or arrested, then … Well, I'd better make do with the …" He looked at his watch. "At the seven minutes and thirteen seconds we have. Closer to six if I want time to make it through the gate."

"Please. Go on."

"Good, then." Maughan looked pleased, but not at all rushed. "I've been told you're on Necrophage?"

"The cure. Yes."

He cocked his head. "It's not a cure, Mrs. Shelton. It's really just a holding pattern. I hope they explained that you'll need to take it for the rest of your life to keep the disease from progressing?"

"They did. I'm sorry. I misspoke."

"Is it working for you? Do you feel you're at the same developmental stage as you were when you came out?"

"How would I feel if it wasn't working?"

"Let's see … it's been about two weeks. The disease seems to have settled at around a three-week development period. After three weeks, you'd basically be a walking corpse … or at least on your way to being one. You don't look two-thirds corpse to me."

"Thank you," Carly said.

"So I'd guess it's working just fine. You understand I have no official ties to Hemisphere, correct?"

"Good. I'd rather not associate with Hemisphere."

"It's not all bad. It was half my company once upon a time and it was noble then, and I daresay that even Archibald Burgess, though he's many things, isn't quite as 'evil' these days. Hemisphere is to thank for the drug that's keeping you human."

"Necrophage," she repeated.

"Precisely." He tapped his crossed-over leg.

"Anyway. Time, time. We should keep moving. May I test your blood?"

"My blood is tested constantly."

"Yes," said Maughan, removing something the size of a wallet, "but as I'm not officially Hemisphere, I'm not officially here. I believe competition is good for development, and I know quite well that you have an axe to grind. See, Necrophage has a base formulation that will keep your disease from worsening, though you will forever be what we're calling 'necrotic.' But there is potential for other formulations in the future. *Better* formulations. So what I'm hoping is that we can make a deal. If you let me sample your blood, I promise to share whatever I develop with you."

"Does it screw Hemisphere?" she asked.

"Definitely."

Carly extended a finger, and he sampled a drop of blood before pocketing the device.

"Well, then." He rose. "It's been wonderful, but our time is already almost up."

"Mr. Maughan?" Carly rose as well.

"Yes?"

"Is it really spreading out there?"

"I'm afraid so. The Bakersfield containment

was not enough. It's no one's fault. Nature has its inevitable ways."

"But Necrophage will stop it."

"We shall see." He turned again, with a smile.

"Mr. Maughan?"

"Yes?"

"Why me?"

"Why you, what?"

"You could take any … *necrotic's* … blood. So why go to all the trouble to come into Mr. Calais's compound to get mine?"

Maughan smiled. "Oh, nobody's told you?"

"Told me what?'

"You are patient zero, in a way."

"I thought it was already named after patient zeroes," Carly told him.

"Yes. 'Sherman' is for Emma Sherman, who first contracted Rip Daddy. 'Pope' was the first to develop the new form. Ergo, the disease is 'Sherman Pope,' and there's no room for 'Sherman Pope Shelton.'"

"That's okay with me," Carly said.

"But you were the first stable case to leave the city. Your virus phenotype was the only survivor. Even Pope died in Bakersfield. Well, 'died.' I guess it's a matter of opinion."

Carly shrugged. "Are they really not going to destroy the city?"

"No need. It's contained, and by now the entire population is necrotic. *Feral*, really, not just necrotic. It was your exit that made them change their minds."

"Why?"

"Because Bakersfield is a petri dish now. It gives them something to study. Maybe a way, in time, to help."

"But that's what I don't understand. Containing Bakersfield did nothing. The virus still got out."

"Ah, yes. But so did you. You are both cause and mitigator in one."

"'Mitigator,'" she repeated.

"I know it's not as sexy as 'cure,' but there is no cure. It will be okay, though, I think. We're simply in for a big change to the world as we know it. We cannot eradicate just yet, so we will contain. I hear they're closing the borders. It will be very interesting, don't you think?"

She could think of a thousand words for what this was, and "interesting" wasn't one of them. Her face must have betrayed her ambivalence because her visitor smiled.

"What will be, will be. It's a much better way to

live than fighting. In my opinion, anyway." He pretended to tip a hat. "Good day, Mrs. Shelton. And thank you."

She dared one final call, now that he was outside her door and halfway down the walk.

He turned, still good-natured, but with a glance at his watch.

"What will it be like, do you think? What's so interesting?"

Maughan smiled even larger. "Come on, now. Lemons into lemonade. Yes, the transition will be hard, but it won't be chaotic like Bakersfield. The Man is already dropping the hammer everywhere. They're forming new government agencies and everything. 'Panacea.' Sounds exciting, doesn't it?"

"But the disease …"

"I know. But look at the upside. A population that's a mix of the living and the dead — doesn't that seem fascinating to you?"

"But will people—?"

"Oh, of course," he said, plucking at the spirit of her question. "People are very adaptable. They can get used to anything — even living next door to people like you, and people much further along in their decay. The internet is already making memes about it. Didn't you know?"

Carly furrowed her brow. "What kind of memes?"

"You haven't heard? Aberdeen Valley, where Hemisphere is moving? You know about the necrotic migration headed that way, don't you?"

"Sure, but …"

Maughan smiled even wider. "And you know what they're calling Aberdeen now, because of it?"

Carly shook her head.

"They're calling it *Dead City*."

THE END

Bakersfield was only the beginning.

As your next read — *Dead City* — begins, Bakersfield is a legend from the past. Panacea thought they stopped the spread of the Rip Daddy virus inside the city's walls, but instead it grew and mutated, becoming the modern-day scourge known as Sherman Pope. Sherman Pope is contained now, but for a while it threatened to undo the world. Only the invention of a drug stopped it from spreading: *Necrophage*, made by the Hemisphere corporation. Thanks to Necrophage, the infected can live among us … or so it seems until a secret is unearthed, and all Hell breaks loose. Read the tale in the biological thriller *Dead City* — the most unique take on zombies you've ever seen.

Right now you can get the *Dead City* for free. Start reading the Dead World trilogy today!

What to read next

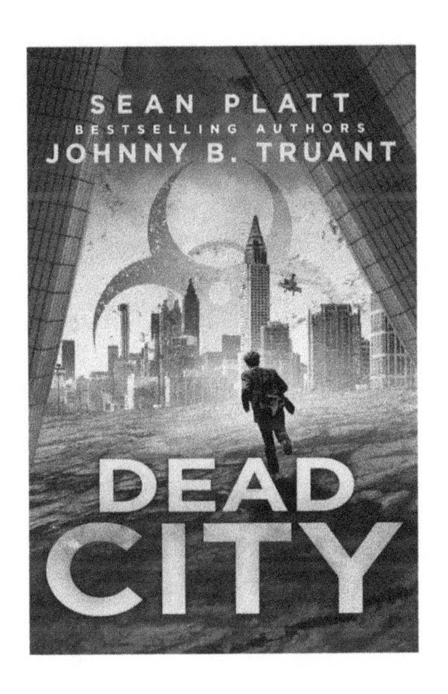

Want to read more about what happens next in the world of *Dead Zero*? You're in luck. Get *Dead City* for free and start the *Dead World Trilogy* today!

Get Dead City Today

A Quick Favor...

If you enjoyed this book, please take a moment to write a short review on your favorite online bookstore so other readers can enjoy it, too.

Thanks so much!
Johnny and Sean

About the Authors

Sean Platt is an entrepreneur and founder of Sterling & Stone, where he makes stories with his partners, Johnny B. Truant, and David W. Wright, and a family of storytellers.

Sean is the bestselling author of over 10 million words' worth of books, including the Yesterday's Gone and Invasion series. Sean is also co-author of the indie publishing cornerstone, Write. Publish. Repeat. and co-host of the Story Studio Podcast.

Originally from Long Beach, California, Sean now lives in Austin, Texas with his wife and two children. He has more than his share of nose.

Johnny B. Truant is co-owner of the Sterling & Stone Story Studio, an IP powerhouse focusing on books and adaptations for film and television. It's the best job in the world, and he spends his days creating cool stuff with partners Sean Platt and

David W. Wright, as well as more than 20 gifted storytellers.

Johnny is the bestselling author of over 100 books under various pen names, including the Fat Vampire and Invasion series. On the nonfiction side, he's also co-author of the indie publishing mainstay Write. Publish. Repeat. and co-host of the weekly Story Studio Podcast.

Originally from Ohio, Johnny and his family now live in Austin, Texas, where he's finally surrounded by creative types as weird as he is.

Lightning Source UK Ltd.
Milton Keynes UK
UKHW010431090223
416681UK00003B/1029